The Good, the Bad and the Mediochre

By Calum P Cameron[1]

[1]   The P stands for
Pneumonoultramicroscopicsilicovolcanoconiosis

For all those at SU camp who seemed so interested.
Especially Rachel since she asked so nicely.

About the Author

Calum P Cameron (the P can stand for whatever you want it to) wrote his first story that could come anywhere near to being called a 'novel' at 15. Subsequently he became very bored and decided to write a second one. He achieved most of his flashes of inspiration while walking the dog, which could account for a lot.

Where exactly he lives is anyone's guess, but his physical form at least seems to spend most of its time in Edinburgh, which could account for even more.

He can usually be found - in body at least - in a modest house in a quiet suburban area with the aforementioned dog, his parents, his sister, his sister's rabbit, and at least seven alter-egos, some of whom he finds quite amusing.

He is aware that he had previously promised several people that he would get a life, but he recently discovered that no-one has ever emerged alive from those things so, at the moment, he's steering well clear of them.

Mediocre (n): Of middling quality, indifferent.
Mediochre (n): Colour, member of red and brown spectra, of position between pale ochre and deep ochre.

A girl stood, leaning against a fence, in the constant drizzle that signified she was in the middle of a Scottish winter. She was wearing a relatively unexciting black and white school uniform; a large blue schoolbag over one shoulder; and a slightly dejected expression.

The monotonous patter of water droplets on pavement was broken by a muffled ringtone. The girl reached into her pocket and removed a mobile phone. She stared blankly at the unfamiliar number who had just texted her, before opening the message. It said:

Run.

Suddenly aware of how dark and quiet it was, and how the wind was faintly rustling the trees nearby in an eerie fashion, the girl glanced left, then right, then, just in case, up. The emptiness was like a deafening scream – there was no-one around.

The phone rang again, and another message from the same number appeared. With a slightly clammy hand, she opened it.

No, really RUN. NOW.

The girl mentally ran through all the people she could think of who might possibly know her number without her knowing theirs, and then narrowed it down to those who would find this sort of thing funny. There *were* a few of those, but most of them were in America. The phone rang a third time, and she opened the message almost before it had appeared.

FOR PITY'S SAKE, WILL YOU JUST GET OUT OF THE WAY?!!!!

Finally, what little rationality had still been clinging to her rattled brain collapsed, and the girl ran, breathing heavily, until she stopped to hyperventilate against a tree.

And without warning, a huge lorry suddenly exploded through the fence she had been leaning against, driving at an insane velocity. She caught a flash of blue, and a suggestion of the words 'Sapphire Storage', and what looked like a wild-eyed driver, far too low in the seat for it to make sense, one hand grappling with the steering wheel and the other holding something small, black and rectangular.

But then the lorry was gone, down the road and around the nearest corner, and the girl had fled.

But that was not the beginning.

***

A large blond man in an immaculate dinner suit stood before another, smaller man, this one with the look of someone who owned all of the immediate area and was perfectly at home, even though he had not in fact ever been in this room before.

"I must say, you're the most useful associate we've got on this team. We could never have brought this operation about without your help," the large man was saying. The smaller man gave a slight nod, as if to say 'of course'.

"In you go then," the large man continued, gesturing towards the heavy oak door to his left. "I daresay Sapphire will have a great many things to discuss with you before it goes ahead."

The small man, without even a second nod, went in, and the larger man let out a breath he had not realised he had been holding.

But that was also not the beginning.

***

A candlestick sat in the middle of a table, illuminating a circle of expensive-looking mahogany. It was tall and gold, but rather plain, the only remarkable feature being the message engraved on it in tiny letters:

> THE FUTURE
> STARTS WITH
> THE PRESENT

The single white candle it held was melting very slowly, and as it did so it gave off the faintest odour of vanilla.

The candle flame *just* revealed the location of several figures seated around the expensive table. There was a suggestion of faces in the darkness, the faint gleam of light bouncing of a pupil, but beyond that none of the occupants of the room could possibly make out any of the other occupants.

A voice that sounded like the sonic equivalent of liquid honey, except slightly crueller, came from one end of the table:

"Then it is agreed. The... Tertiary Phase, if you like, is to be initiated."

A second voice, this one quite obviously that of a woman from Continental Europe, replied softly:

"In which case, which of them are to be doing the initiating?"

The first voice, the one that sounded like a knife-edged caress, responded:

"I think that is a... matter for the parties themselves."

To which another voice, one that bore traces of every accent known to man and several unknown, yet unidentifiable as actually being any of them, spoke with less emotion than the Speaking Clock.

"I believe *I* would be the most suited for this particular job. Unless there are any objections."

Which, as it turned out, there were not, and so the meeting was terminated, the candle blown out and each occupant departed via a different door in the blackness.

But that was still not the beginning.

***

A large iron sword, with serrated edges and a heavy ornate handle, tore its way through scales and skin and sinew, even taking a chunk out of the bone, so powerful was its swipe and so furious the arm behind it.

Blood gushed. There was a final rattling cross between a scream and a cough, and then eyes clouded and head fell limp, still with thick, deep redness leaching out of the wound.

Far away, behind a convenient rock outcrop, a terrified woman tried to stifle the cry of despair and terror threatening to burst from her lungs, and shrank further into the shadows.

But, while it was certainly a turning point, that was not the beginning either.

***

On a temporary wooden platform on the side of a half-finished building, a young man clung to a piece of ornamentation on the wall for support and yelled above the clamouring gale:

"Pass me that hammer over here, quick!"

To which his workmate replied:

"Quoi?"

Even that cannot be said to have been the true beginning, but exactly what happened before that nobody knows anyway. Beginnings are tricky. No matter how far back you go, which event you pick, there will always have been at least one previous event which caused that event to occur.

Life is a little like a story, but it's a story where the first seven or so chapters have been lost and it's not even possible to work out exactly what happened in them from the clues throughout the rest of it. Life cannot be easily divided into a beginning, middle and end; it just has one long middle where all the subplots and characters keep changing, up until the point of death. And then the story gets *really* complicated.

But whatever the beginning may have been, it was the *end* which people remembered. Partly because it was the only bit most people ever found out about, partly because it happened so much faster than the rest of it, and partly because it had more explosions. People are like that, and probably have been since the very beginning. But, of course, we can't be sure about that until someone finds those first seven chapters.

***

The end started on a rather ordinary day in early spring, in a school playground somewhere in Edinburgh. Charlotte Johnson was leaning against a wall, her long darkish-blonde hair almost obscuring her gloomy expression. She wanted to go home. Really home. She had wanted to go home for several months now. She had never really liked Edinburgh. They had a law, an actual *law* to prevent buildings being over four floors high; their education system was, frankly, nuts; and after a while their accent ceased to be a novelty and became a mere irritation.

Of course, home, her *real* home, the town in Florida where she had grown up, hadn't had many buildings over four floors high either; and she hadn't particularly liked their education system all that much at the time. But it was the *principle* of the thing. And at least they all talked in accents you could understand.

But the chances of her actually *getting* home at any point in the near future seemed to be somewhere below those of Hell freezing over and opening a successful ski resort.

The worst part, the really *worst* part, was that nobody else seemed to *notice* how bad this city was. Her parents both seemed perfectly happy, and obviously none of the locals could see what was wrong. They hadn't even believed her about the lorry incident last winter. She had eventually given up trying to explain before her mother decided to punish her for trying to ruin their new life or something.

The lorry incident. Something had reminded her of the lorry incident there. She didn't know exactly how she knew, but she could tell that there was something... something *nearby*...

There. There was a boy, possibly as old as her, probably slightly younger, running up the schoolground steps to her left with the expression of someone who has somewhere important to be in a few minutes, and doesn't really approve of all these kids in the way.

He was the most bizarrely-dressed person Charlotte thought she had ever seen in her life. He was wearing a shirt and pants - sorry, *trousers* - made of some kind of yellow-brown leather with thousands of pockets; some sort of thick, heavy, dark brown body-warmer over that; a pair of what looked like black hiking boots; and a khaki camouflage-print sunhat with a fairly wide brim. The overall effect was to make him look like a ridiculous attempt at a desert soldier. What she recognised about him, though, was the face. The last time she had seen it, it had been hurtling past her at an absurd speed, but the image had burnt itself onto her mental retina. The shock of dark brown hair, too short to be long for a boy, but still longer than a boy's hair usually is. The jade-green eyes. The expression that indicated that part of his brain was worried while another part was finding this all rather amusing. The constant impression that he was *calculating* something. None of this she could have remembered if asked to describe the driver of the Sapphire Storage lorry, but now that it was there, darting up her playground steps, it was shockingly familiar.

It could all be coincidence, of course. The rational part of her mind told her that this was silly; she couldn't recognise someone she'd hardly seen for a second, if that.

But then the boy glanced in her direction. And his expression suddenly went from '*Come on, I've got to be there soon*' to '*Oh my gosh, that's HER.*'

Well that was it. Suddenly this outlandish boy represented for her all that was wrong with this whole stupid country. She hoisted her schoolbag onto her shoulder and ran after him. The boy looked at her, then glanced up towards the school, then back at her. He seemed to reach a decision, and ran on. Charlotte scowled and sped up.

She followed the boy through the foyer, into the concourse, and down the steps to the maths department, before losing him completely. Too angry to give up now, she sprinted through the department, glancing through the glass pane of every sickly green door as she passed. Empty, empty, empty, empty apart from a teacher who clearly didn't get enough of her classroom while teaching in it or something, empty...

Then the loud thud of something heavy falling over made her slow down slightly, and cautiously peer through the next doorway. The boy was standing inside, leaning against the opposite wall, one hand idly throwing and catching a graphics calculator. He would catch it at one end, allow its weight to swing his hand downwards at the wrist, and then flick it sharply upwards, letting go of the calculator as he did so, causing the latter to turn on its axis in the air – once, twice, three-and-a-half times – before catching it again. He would have given the impression of carefree nonchalance, had it not been for the ugly black handgun being pointed at the middle of his face, which his eyes were almost crossed trying to focus on.

On the other end of the gun was a black-haired woman wearing a black silk suit and gloves, her long hair hiding her face from Charlotte's viewing angle and giving the impression of a pillar of pure night with added weaponry. She was speaking very quietly. Between them was a table on its side, presumably knocked over as she advanced on the boy. Charlotte made a small sound somewhere between a gasp and a gag.

The woman spun around, pointing the weapon straight at Charlotte. At the exact same time, the boy raised the calculator above his head. The woman, apparently somehow sensing the raised calculator, dived and rolled aside, springing to her feet and raising the gun at the doorway again, but in the time it took her to perform such a manoeuvre the boy had run across the room, dropping the calculator as he did so, grabbed Charlotte's arm and dragged her down the corridor with his own momentum.

"We've really got to stop meeting like this," the boy grinned as they pelted around the corner with the sound of running footsteps behind them. In some strange way, he seemed to be almost enjoying the fact that he was currently being chased by an armed assassin. Charlotte gasped, momentarily stunned at the casualness with which he confessed to being the driver that had almost killed her three months ago. The boy seemed not to notice.

"Which way's the quickest exit?" he asked.

"Left," Charlotte managed to say after she'd regained full use of her tongue. The boy smiled again and, without slowing down, grabbed her arm once more and hauled her down the right corridor. "What are you doing?" she hissed as she was dragged up the stairs back into the concourse.

"Well," said the boy calmly as they ran towards the door back into the foyer, "if *I* was an intelligent, trained killer – God forbid – I'd be leaping out from a side corridor in front of the door down there so as to cut off the escapees as they tried to get out, right about... now. Come on." He pushed open the concourse door and ran straight into it as it was pushed back towards him by a man in a suit who had up until that point been leaning against the wall beside it trying to look like a teacher.

Charlotte stifled a yelp and turned to run in the opposite direction as the boy reeled back clutching at his nose, but stopped suddenly when the floor tile in front of her exploded into fragments. Looking up, she saw the black-clad woman from earlier running through the door at the opposite end of the concourse, her unwavering hand pointing the firearm straight at Charlotte. A further three men and one woman, all clad in the same black silk, emerged from various doors or, in one man's case, from a rubbish bin beside Charlotte, flicking a banana peel from his shoulder as he did so. They were all armed. Charlotte could feel herself starting to practically hyperventilate.

The fake teacher advanced slowly on the boy, who had just recovered. He smiled slightly, like a snooker player whose opponent has just accidently set him up for the perfect shot.

"You have something belonging to us, I believe," he said quietly, holding out his hand, palm upwards. Charlotte noticed for the first time that there was a sizeable bulge in the boy's leather body-warmer.

"Do I?" said the boy, frowning. "Nope. I don't think so. Let's see..." He unzipped the body-warmer and began pulling various items from various pockets. "One packet of hankies, bought from a corner shop... one parker ball-point pen with my name engraved on it, that was a present... one small broken pencil, I think I took that from the University... one mobile phone, bought years ago for a fiver... one set of keys, all of which are mine... one wallet - I think Joseph bought me that after he lost my old one - containing fifteen pounds plus change, all of which I earned, and various identification cards, all of which I was given... oh, and one glittering egg which I believe I liberated from the thieves who were planning to sell it illegally..." He held up a smooth round sphere, about the size of an ostrich egg, which glinted blue in the light.

The fake teacher smiled coldly. "Well done. A point well made. Now, hand it over. In case you think you can get out of it somehow, I would like to draw your attention to the three guns currently pointed at you and the further two pointed at your girlfriend."

The boy looked the fake teacher in the sneer, not being tall enough to look him in the eye. "Technically, we've only *really* known each other for about two minutes. And I'm *not* talking biblically, or like '*The Crucible*'. Sorry, that joke was clearly wasted on you. Unfortunately, I do have this phobia of seeing innocent people being shot." He placed the sphere carefully in the fake teacher's hand, causing the latter's sneer to widen still further.

"Is that really it? I thought we were supposed to be facing the great Mediochre Q Seth, who once held off a horde of Undead with his teeth, and brought down the world's biggest dragon-slaying organisation with a single blow? Aren't you going to fight?"

"Well, I'd like to," said the boy, his expression blanker than that of the whitewashed concourse wall. "Really I would. But I had this operation recently. On my clavichord."

"A rarely used musical instrument similar to a piano?" said one of the black-clad men, raising an eyebrow.

"J.D Salinger's '*The Catcher in the Rye*', Chapter 13. Holden Caulfield to Sunny," said a voice behind Charlotte, as something cold and hard pressed lightly against the back of her neck. The boy merely smiled slightly. Then, suddenly, he said:

"Actually, now that I come to think of it, I do have some of your stuff in here." He was speaking very quickly, pulling things from deep pockets and tossing them to the armed guards around him, all of whom caught them instinctively.

"One stapler, three packets of staples, one box of pencils, one gun cartridge, and one calculator." This last was thrown to the woman behind Charlotte, who had to remove her gun from the back of Charlotte's head to catch it. "*And* one spontaneous mantic ignition organ, commonly known as a fire gland *if any of you moves your arms I will crush it!*" He had stepped back into a position where he could see all of the armed people and was now holding a large, organic-looking silver blob, very carefully, in his fist. The armed men and women, each with their gun no longer pointed at anyone since they had moved their arms to catch what they'd been thrown, had frozen and were each eying the blob or the boy's expression nervously.

"Now," said the boy quietly, "the young woman is going to leave. You will not attempt to stop this."

He jerked his head in the direction of the door and Charlotte ran through it, through the foyer and out into the grounds, meanwhile removing her mobile from her pocket. She got as far as the first two nines before she noticed that there was something wrong. Everyone out in the grounds was too still, and now that she looked closely there were leaves and pieces of litter hovering slightly above the ground. She tried to stop, but unfortunately her momentum forced her to take one step to many.

"Richty-ho then," said the boy called Mediochre Q Seth, exaggerating his own Scottish accent. "If you would be so kind as to drop your weapons without moving any more than necessary." There was a series of clatters. "And *now*, sir, I believe *you* have something which, while not actually mine, I would very much like to have returned to my custody." The fake teacher handed over the glittering egg. Still holding the fire gland, Mediochre tucked it back into his body-warmer; picked up the assorted weaponry lying around; removed the ammo from each; stashed it in various pockets; dropped the empty weapons into a bin; briefly searched the now-unarmed gunpeople; removed any spare ammo they had; stashed that away as well; then finally stood behind the group and said, in as polite a voice as he could, "You may now move, but only forwards, towards the exit. I will walk behind you, still with this here little gland, because of course I wouldn't want it to fall into the wrong hands."

They marched through the foyer and out into the grounds, whereupon the first two rows suddenly froze. All that was left were Mediochre, the fake teacher and the woman who had cornered him originally.

"Ooh. Original," said Mediochre. "Tempomancy in a ring around the school. Not seen that one before." He raised his voice. "Oi! Mr-slash-Miss-slash-Other Tempomancer! I have here a –"

At which point the woman whirled her wrist in a strange arc while snapping her fingers and a small fireball shot out of her hand and singed Mediochre's fingers, causing him to drop the gland, which she then placed a foot over gently. Mediochre could tell what she was thinking. It had been a pretty good threat when the only people being blown up would be himself, them and one girl he didn't know, because the egg, which they'd known he cared about, would survive. But no-one would be stupid enough to believe someone would let the gland explode in the middle of a child-packed playground. Unless the someone in question were a generally-immoral smuggler or something like that.

"I *had* here a spontaneous mantic ignition organ or fire gland," he said, hardly missing a beat, "which I *was* going to use to threaten you until you put time back to normal, but it now appears to be in the hands of your pyromancer friend who is currently rubbing her fingers together in a threatening way, so don't bother, I'm giving her the egg." He tossed the egg as hard as he could at the pyromancer woman, who caught it but had to take a step back due to the force he'd thrown it at. A step which brought her into the ring of stopped time.

Mediochre casually reached out and plucked the egg from her hands, which were currently unable to resist since the nerve signal saying 'What do I do now?' froze when it got about half way up the forearm. That just left him, the fake teacher and the unseen tempomancer.

He turned to the fake teacher, to be met with the smirk of someone who's about to reveal a winning hand. Mediochre looked down. There was a small but noticeably gun-like black shape in the man's hand.

"Say hello to my little friend," the man drawled, giving Mediochre the distinct impression that he practiced that line every night just in case he ever got to use it. Mediochre gave a huge, friendly grin.

"Hello, little friend! I have a little friend too!" he smiled, and shook his arm slightly. A small, brown, long-tailed fieldmouse hopped out of his sleeve and onto the man's hand. The man stared. "This is Desra," said Mediochre helpfully. "She's a mouse," he added. The man snarled and pulled the trigger. Nothing happened. He looked, and saw that the safety had been turned on again.

"What the –" he said, before yelping and dropping the gun as Desra sank small but sharp teeth into his hand. Mediochre caught it before it hit the ground and pressed it against the man's forehead.

"I believe you're already friends, so I won't bother introducing you," he said. The man crossed his eyes in an effort to see the gun.

"Are you holding that thing *backwards?*" he asked, leaning back so he could see.

"Probably," said Mediochre. "I'm not at home around firearms." And with that he jabbed the man between the eyes with the butt of the gun, causing him to overbalance and fall. He didn't hit the ground.

Mediochre tucked the egg securely back into his body-warmer again, and let Desra crawl up his sleeve once more. "So," he said to the air. "*Now will you turn off your tempomantic ring?*"

Charlotte felt a hand on her shoulder and turned around. The boy was standing behind her, grinning.

"There we are. All back to normal. Now would be a good time to run like the blazes."

They did. So did the crowds of schoolchildren who had suddenly seen a group of angry, black-clad ex-gunpeople appear from nowhere, two of said gunpeople falling over as they did so. Unfortunately, not all of the schoolchildren were running away in the same direction. And, as any mainstream school pupil can tell you, trying to run after someone when there's a crowd of scared and/or rowdy schoolchildren pushing and jostling between you and them is never going to work.

Eventually, the crowd cleared, leaving the ex-gunpeople, all now standing up, staring around themselves trying to work out which way the two they were after had gone. The pyromancer turned a glare like the fires of Hell on the fake teacher.

"You let him get away when you were the only one armed?" she hissed. The fake schoolteacher tried to protest, before realising how lame an excuse 'His mouse bit me' would be. The pyromancer snarled, and shot a small ball of flame at the fake teacher's face. The fake teacher stumbled backwards and fell over again.

And landed on the fire gland, which was still lying innocently where it had been dropped.

Everyone in the grounds heard the explosion; even those who couldn't see the plume of white flame and sparks flaring up into the sky. Basic instinct took over and they commenced to run around yelling and generally not having any idea as to what was happening or what to do. Through the uncomprehending multitude, Charlotte and the boy ran towards the school gates.

"What was that?" yelled Charlotte over the throng.

"I don't know for certain," replied the boy, "But it came from the direction of the people we're running from, so it almost definitely isn't good!"

"But what... what if they... what if someone's hurt?" Charlotte replied, but the by shook his head.

"These aren't the kind of people to hang around killing innocents when their quarry's currently making for their car."

"WHAT?" screamed Charlotte, the small part of her brain that was still functioning normally wondering whether she'd gone mad or if it was just the rest of the world. The boy raised an eyebrow.

"Do I *look* old enough to own a car? No. I am, but that's beside the point. And I don't fancy waiting around for a bus, and I can't run all that far or fast compared to these guys. So that leaves only one feasible option." It was probably the rest of the world, thought Charlotte. She doubted if, even when insane, her mind could dream up something this weird.

When they reached the exit, there was indeed a nondescript black car sitting outside. The words 'Sapphire Storage' were written on the bonnet. Had Charlotte not already concluded that the world had gone mad, she probably would have freaked out. The boy walked up to the driver's-side door, and removed a small, black, roughly-cuboid shaped object from his pocket. It looked uncannily like an out-of-date mobile phone, of the kind that hadn't been made for years. It even had 'Nokia' written across the top.

"Chips?" he said quietly. The screen lit up. "Unlock." The phone bleeped. The boy typed in a number. The phone bleeped again. There was a slight pause. Then, without warning, the car unlocked itself. The engine even started running.

"How –" Charlotte began, but another voice cut her off.

"I do hope you aren't stealing from our company *again*," it said. Charlotte and the boy both turned. The woman who had originally cornered him was advancing on the boy. She clicked her fingers, and her hand suddenly burst into flame. Charlotte screamed, but the woman seemed not to care.

"What happened?" asked the boy, glancing around.

"I'm afraid there was a little... accident," said the woman, still advancing. "My... associates were too close when it happened. As indeed was I, but as you may have noticed I have a certain... *way* with flames."

"I had noted that, actually. Spontaneous mantic ignition upon fillip. Very good. Nowhere near as impressive as when a *dragon* does it, of course. But, look, can we talk about this?"

The woman didn't even reply. She just thrust the flame at the boy, who caught it full in the head and recoiled, clutching at his face. Then, after a few moments, he sighed, straightened up again and removed his hands. His face was remarkably un-charred, although the same could not be said of his fringe.

"That was my *hair*, you flamethrowing hag," he said indignantly. The woman clicked the fingers of both her hands at the same time, then thrust them both outwards with the palms facing the boy. Twin jets of flame erupted from her hands and engulfed the boy's head and shoulders. The force blasted him backwards into the car, and he collapsed against it, falling to the ground. Charlotte could smell burnt meat.

The flamethrower woman turned to advance upon Charlotte, smirking cruelly. Charlotte began to back away, trying desperately to think of a way out. The woman raised her hands very slowly in front of her, and clicked her fingers. Two yellow-white flames sprang up, inches from Charlotte's face. And then from behind the woman came the sound of a throat being cleared.

"*I... liked... that... hair*," growled an angry voice. The flamethrowing woman spun around. The boy was standing behind her. There were faint burn marks on his skin, but they were slowly disappearing. The front of his hair was on fire. The woman opened her mouth, but no sound came out. "Yes," said the boy quietly. "When it comes to freaky powers, I *do* beat you hands down."

At which point Charlotte landed on the woman's back, the large stone she had picked up connecting sharply with the back of the woman's head.

"So," said the boy as he drove through the streets of Edinburgh in the inconspicuous black car, Charlotte in the passenger's seat and the pyromancer tied up in the back with some metal chains the boy had managed to find somewhere. "Anything you want to ask me?"

Charlotte had refused point-blank to go back to the school and get ticked off at the fire assembly point until the boy had explained what was going on, and he had eventually given up trying to argue and told her to get in the car. Now she tried to get her thoughts in order.

"Right," she said. "First thing's first." There was a pause.

"Well?" said the boy after a while.

"I'm trying to work out which of the many things flying around inside my head counts as the first thing."

"How about 'Who are you?'; that's usually a good place to start," said the boy kindly.

"Right," said Charlotte again. "Yes. Good. WHO THE HELL ARE YOU?"

"No need to shout," said the boy, flinching away from her slightly. "Besides, that man in the school introduced me, remember? I'm Mediochre Q Seth." Charlotte raised an eyebrow.

"Your parents not have very many hopes for you?" she asked. The boy looked unimpressed.

"Actually, it's a shade of brownish-red. Not as dark as deep ochre but darker than pale ochre. And my parents didn't choose it; I did."

"So what's your *real* name, then?" asked Charlotte, starting to get irritated. Just for a second, the boy looked uncomfortable, as if she'd asked him a terribly personal question about his family life or something.

"We, er, don't like to tell people unless they're *really* close to us. It's silly really, an old superstition, but there was this time... we don't like to talk about that either."

"Who's 'we'?" demanded Charlotte.

"The Mantically Aware. Commonly known as the Knowers."

"Mantically aware?" asked Charlotte, now definitely annoyed. The boy who called himself Mediochre nodded, seeming not to notice.

"Yep. *Lit*: 'those who are aware of the existence of magic, or mancy as it is properly called'. As opposed to the Mantically Unaware, or the Ignorants."

"So now there's such thing as magic, too?" asked Charlotte scathingly. Mediochre only raised an eyebrow at her in a very irksome way.

"You did *see* those flames come out of a human being's hands, didn't you?" he asked, even more scathingly. Charlotte suppressed the urge to insult or slap him.

"And, the way your burns healed up so quickly... was that magic too?" she asked. Mediochre seemed to dither slightly.

"Ye-es. No. Not exactly. Well, basically. I was involved in a... a sort of magical accident a long time ago. Since then I've had, sort of, regenerative qualities. Like a starfish. Cut bits off, they grow back, sort of thing."

"What kind of magical accident?" asked Charlotte, curiosity overcoming her frustration. Mediochre shuffled slightly in his seat, not taking his eyes off of the road.

"I don't talk about that much."

"There's a lot you don't talk about, isn't there?" said Charlotte harshly. "Ok, how long ago was it? How old were you?"

"Fifty," said Mediochre. Charlotte narrowed her eyebrows.

"I'm not laughing," she said.

"Nor am I," said Mediochre quietly. There were a few moments of silence before he eventually spoke again. "Look, it's like... did you ever do recurrence relations in maths? $U_{(n+1)}=aU_n+b$ *et cetera*?" Charlotte's ravaged brain stirred around until her memory threw up something like this from a math lesson years ago.

"Uh...huh..." she said, uncertainly. This seemed to be enough for Mediochre.

"Well, from the point of the... accident, my age hasn't gone like a simple '$U_{(n+1)}=1U_n+1$' each year, which is the norm, but instead, because of the regenerative properties, it goes '$U_{(n+1)}= \frac{14}{15} U_n+1$'." Charlotte stared in a nonplussed manner.

"In other words, every year, as well as getting one year older, my biological age also decreased by one-fifteenth. Which, if you work it out, means that starting from the accident my age has decreased until it hit 15, whereupon it remains pretty much the same."

"So... you're, like, a 90-year-old in a 15-year-old's body?" hazarded Charlotte.

"You've grasped the basic idea," said Mediochre grimly.

"Right..." Charlotte tried to think of what to ask next. "What happened three months ago? I got these texts, and then –"

"Aha!" exclaimed Mediochre brightly. "That was little Chips here." He removed the ancient mobile from his pocket. Charlotte stared at it uncomprehendingly. Mediochre sighed.

"Some people just don't recognise great mancy when they see it. Chips here is an IMP. That's 'Intrusively Mantic 'Phone'. A technomancer friend of mine makes them. Anything that works by some sort of wave signal, unless blocked, an IMP can hack into, provided the owner has clearance. Unless the owner is me, in which case the IMP thinks I have clearance for everything. My friend made sure of that when he put them into production. I got Chips to hack into any other mobiles in my path and leave those texts, so's no-one would get hurt. I also, you may have noticed, used him to unlock the car I'm driving." Charlotte's brain was already beginning to ache with the sheer scale of the new information it was receiving.

"What's a technomancer?" she asked.

"A type of mage," explained Mediochre. "Technomancy is technology-magic. Pyromancy, like our unconscious friend back there, is fire-magic. There's also tempomancy, hydromancy, medimancy, phobiamancy..."

"Necromancy?" Charlotte chipped in.

"Not anymore," said Mediochre. "Not in this country at least. The Queen banned it."

"The *Queen* knows about –" Charlotte began, but Mediochre waved her into silence.

"Not *that* queen. Mantically-Aware Britain has its own separate government to deal with matters the normal government doesn't know about. The current Prime Minister of that government is called Kathryn Queen, better known as Queen MAB." He grinned. Charlotte looked blank. "As in, 'Then I see Queen Mab has been with you...'" he explained. Charlotte still looked blank. "Romeo and Juliet?" he proffered.

"Oh," said Charlotte. "I've never read that." Mediochre rolled his eyes.

"Anything else you'd like to ask?" he said.

"Yeah," replied Charlotte, "Where are we going?"

"Well, first we're going to see some people from the government I told you about so that I can tell people about Sapphire Storage. Then I'm taking you back to school. No arguments."

"Who the hell are Sapphire Storage?" said Charlotte, wondering to herself why she hadn't asked that sooner.

"Aha," smiled Mediochre, stopping the car. "*That's* a good question. And it's one you're about to find out the answer to, Miss... Hang on a minute, who *are* you?"

"Charlotte," said Charlotte. "Charlotte Johnson."

"I see," said Mediochre, opening the car door. "Delighted to have met you, Miss Charlotte Charlotte Johnson."

They were parked in an empty street next to a slightly run-down red brick house. It was pretty much indistinguishable from the slightly run-down house to its left, or the slightly run-down house to its right, or indeed any of the houses around the area which were in varying states of slightly run-downedness. Charlotte had to wonder how anyone knew which house to go into – it didn't even have a number above the door.

The door wasn't locked, but just inside it was a very solid-looking brick wall, with what appeared to be a small microphone embedded in it.

Mediochre tapped the microphone twice, waited a while, and then tapped it again. A calm woman's voice similar to that of a satellite navigation system came out of nowhere.

"Please state name now, Sir, Madam or Other."

"Dr Mediochre Quirinius Seth," said Mediochre. There was a pause before the sat-nav voice spoke again.

"Name not recognised. Please amend and state again." Mediochre sighed loudly.

"Professor Doctor Laird Sir Mediochre Quirinius Seth, PhD MusD MSc CBE OBE MIMC VC-Bar, and I also have a Grade 8 in piano if you want to know," he said, somewhat sardonically. There was another slight pause.

"Go right in, Sir. Congratulations on your musical ability," said the voice, without even a hint of detectable sarcasm.

Inside the house, there was just one huge, lavishly-decorated room, with a stage full of chairs, each with their little desk and microphone, at one end and a long buffet table at either side. Four crystal chandeliers hung from the ceiling, casting rainbows of luminosity over everything. The walls were a pale blue with a pattern of silver griffins.

And it was packed with people shouting and arguing and generally failing to be heard above the throng. Mediochre rolled his eyes and removed a metal spork from a pocket. He moved over to one of the buffet tables, tapped a large man in an expensive tuxedo on the back, and spoke to him. The man took the spork, moved a platter of cheese out of the way, and walloped the spork repeatedly off the table, making a noise so loud that everyone in the room stopped talking and turned to face him. Mediochre took the spork gently from his hand, climbed up onto the tabletop, and spoke.

"Would someone like to tell me what's going on in here?"

It eventually transpired that the row had been about worldwide illegal smuggling levels, which had apparently risen to twice as high as they had been in living memory, and the fact that it appeared the vast majority of the smuggling was being carried out by a group called the Sapphire Smuggling Syndicate. From what Charlotte picked up from the debate, the SSS had been smuggling magical contraband from all over the world to paying customers in a variety of countries, and the heightened security measures put in place by the magical governments of these countries appeared to be having roughly as much effect as the average dead termite.

At this point, Mediochre ran a hand through his slightly-singed hair and turned to the group of important-looking men and women on the stage, who appeared to be the local division of Great Britain's magical government, and said gravely:

"What *kind* of magical contraband might this be?" although it seemed he already knew what answer to expect.

"Dragon parts," intoned a tall, grey-haired gentleman in a grey and black pinstripe suit. Mediochre let out a long breath.

"Right. In that case, I'll be brief. The Sapphire Storage Facility *really is* run by the SSS. It makes sense, really. When you're looking for a company as clever as them, somewhere with a similar name is the *last* place you expect to find them, which logically means it's the first place they go. And, as I'm sure you don't need me to tell you, the most likely situation by..." he paused, as if thinking, "...well, I won't bore you with figures, but it's an *awful* lot... is that they're behind the recent increase in slayings. Which means they must have at least one hired slayer working for them, probably many more due to the sheer number of deaths. And in *that* case, I'm upgrading my case to include this whole thing. Any one of you try and stop me and you don't even want to *know* how painful the rest of your life will be."

He was speaking very calmly, but is eyes were full of barely-contained fury. The old grey man glanced at his peers before saying:

"Very well. You have our permission to run this investigation. All help you require will be given as requested wherever possible." Mediochre nodded.

"Darn straight," he said, grabbed Charlotte's arm, and left. "Carry on, Jimmy!" he yelled as he closed the door behind himself.

Mediochre slammed the car door and spoke without looking at Charlotte. "You're going back to school now, Miss Johnson. I have more important things to deal with and I expect you're being missed." Charlotte folded her arms.

"No I am not. These Sapphire people have almost killed me and I want answers." Mediochre narrowed his eyes.

"I don't have time for this. You're going back, end of," he said, starting the car.

"You can't make me," said Charlotte. It sounded immature, she knew, but it was true – technically speaking he had no authority over her, *and* she was bigger than him. Mediochre sighed exasperatedly and ran a hand through his untidy hair.

"I don't know how your mother gets you up in the mornings, but the woman deserves a medal," he said. "All right, I'll explain things as best I can as we drive. There's an old friend I need to speak to. You can come along for the ride, but after that I'm leaving you whether you let me drive you back to school or not. And trust me; the friend in question *can* make you leave. He's done it before with bigger, more *armed* people than you." He stood on the accelerator and the car began to move.

"Right," said Charlotte. "Start at the top, beginning with who you are and why you're going after these people."

"I'm a dracologist," was Mediochre's answer. Charlotte had never had much of an interest in trying to learn Latin, but some words she had managed to pick up from day-to-day living.

"You study dragons?" she said disbelievingly. Mediochre rolled his eyes.

"That *is* the conventional definition of 'dracology', yes," he said. Charlotte managed to resist hitting him and instead snapped:

"So what are you doing in Scotland?" One of Mediochre's eyebrows vanished into his disorderly hair.

"Good dragon country," he said, as though explaining the obvious. "I mean, if you just want to see a dragon, any dragon, then China or Thailand's a better bet, but for a proper, wings-and-flames European dragon, you can't see much better than good old Scotia." Charlotte became aware that she was mouthing soundlessly and stopped.

"But...but... I thought dragons lived in caves on snowy mountains and... stuff," she said, somewhat lamely. Mediochre merely grinned.

"Ever been to a place called Aveimore? Ask the locals, they'll be able to point out the nearest snowy mountain caves if you like." Charlotte lapsed into silence, before eventually speaking again.

"So... you study dragons for money? And that's why you live here?" Mediochre bit his lip thoughtfully.

"Well... yes, although field dracology isn't all that profitable nowadays, so I also lecture in it and work as a slayer-catcher on the side. And it was while studying one particular dragon several months ago that I came across a branch of the Sapphire Smuggling Syndicate that was planning to steal and sell said dragon's eggs." Charlotte's brain was working hard to keep up; she really wished the day would stop throwing revelations at her quite so *fast*.

"And a slayer catcher... catches dragon slayers?"

"Yep," said Mediochre proudly. "And any other illegal monster-slayers around, but I personally specialize in those of a scaly-winged nature." Charlotte could almost feel the hysteria trying to force its way into her mind: *this cannot physically be the truth, because it's too weird.*

"This is starting to sound very *Indiana Jones*," she said. At that, Mediochre thoughtfully removed his camouflage-print sunhat with one hand and looked at it, while somehow still managing to steer the car.

"I think I would need a bigger hat," he remarked.

"And a whip," replied Charlotte absent-mindedly, trying to work out what the tiny fact that was suddenly niggling at her mind actually *was*. Mediochre nodded thoughtfully.

"That too," he said. "How do you actually *use* a whip? Is it all in the wrist or what?" Charlotte gave him a scathing look.

"How exactly would *I* know?" she asked. Then, suddenly, she realised what the niggling was. "Back in that... government place thing, did you *really* manage to work out those exact odds in a few seconds, or did you already know?" Mediochre said nothing for several moments, and the silence in the car seemed almost solid, like it was crushing her. The sensation was not relieved when he finally spoke.

"Did you ever hear of that man, a few years ago, who woke up from a coma to find his piano-playing was miraculously improved from before? Well... I don't know, maybe it was something like that, but after my... accident, it wasn't *just* my body that was working differently. I suddenly saw the world in a different way. It was like... everything ultimately came down to numbers all of a sudden, and all you had to do was count them up as you saw them. Even human emotion. I could read an Agatha Christie novel and by the third or fourth chapter I knew who was the murderer and why, just by putting a lot of two-and-twos together. I was suddenly an expert at chess, purely because I could tell which course of action my opponent was most likely to take. At first I found it amazing, a gift, but after a while it just gets ... depressing, in a way. It's like Cassandra from Greek Mythology – I can work out what's going to happen well before anyone else, and half the time I still can't stop it, not without starting something worse. And as well as that... you can't imagine what it's like and I can't explain it.

But having all of God's creation mapped out in front of you in *equations*... Believe me, Charlotte; you don't ever want to see that. It's just... too weird."

All of a sudden Charlotte couldn't think of anything more to say. The rest of the car journey passed in silence, while in the confused tangle of her brain, Mediochre's words kept shouldering their way between the jumble of new facts already milling around aimlessly.

When at last the car stopped, Mediochre's mood seemed to have lightened. You could say this for the man – he seemed able to bounce back from anything. He got out of the car, and didn't seem to object when Charlotte followed suit. They were in the car park of a huge building, made from reddish stone except for several more modern add-ons of wood and metal. An engraving above the huge black doors read:

St Merlin's University
Of
Mantically-Aware Britain
Founded 1722

"Since when was Merlin a saint?" asked Charlotte. Mediochre glanced upwards at the engraved words as they walked towards the doors beneath.

"Different Merlin," he said simply, before removing his wallet from the depths of his leather attire and taking out an identification card, which he then swiped through a slot beside the doors. Like in the previous building, a voice spoke from nowhere, but this time it was that of a friendly-sounding female with a strong Scottish accent.

"Hi there, welcome to St Merlin's; you're being spoken at by the disembodied voice of Dean Kiwi Mashuga. Who are ya and what're ya here for?" it asked. Mediochre smiled slightly and rolled his eyes.

"Dr Mediochre Quirinius Seth, Lecturer in Dracology. I have a bunch of extra bits around the name and a Grade 8 in piano, but most people ignore that bit. I'm here to see Professor Carrion," he said, much less formally than he had been with the last one.

"Gotcha, Dr Red. He's in the cafe to your right," replied the disembodied voice of the Dean, as the doors swung inwards and Mediochre and Charlotte stepped inside.

"Kiwi's just a wee bit eccentric," Mediochre explained as they walked in, "but we haven't had a better Dean in at least eighty years. Don't tell her I said that."

He opened a door to their right, and they walked into a small cafe with little wooden tables, large green armchairs and a general feeling of pleasant ambience. At a table near the back of the room was a lean, handsome, dark-haired man in his twenties wearing an outfit composed entirely from black: t-shirt, jeans, belt, even his long coat was the colour of charcoal. Charlotte couldn't help noticing as they got closer that his jet-black belt had a jet-black gun holster attached to it, although it was, to her relief, empty.

He appeared to be talking to himself, and it was only when they were slightly nearer that Charlotte noticed there was a second occupant to the table – she wasn't hard to see once you realised she was there, but something about her seemed to make her hard to notice from a distance. Probably magic again, thought Charlotte, somewhat cynically. Now that she could see her, Charlotte studied the other woman. She looked as if she ought to be easier to notice – she was unusually tall, slim and pale-skinned, like she rarely entered the sunlight. She was also wearing some sort of bizarre cross between a leather jacket and a robe which reached down to below her knees, and had as many pockets down the front of it as Mediochre had in his entire get-up. Her coppery reddish-brown bob seemed distinctly out-of-place above her pale striking features and scarily green eyes with streaks of gold through them.

Looking at those eyes sent a chill down Charlotte's spine, and she quickly turned back to the man in black. He had seen them now, and his face had lit up with recognition.

"Medi!" he said, rising from his seat to greet Mediochre. He had a faint English accent, like a Londoner who had been living in Scotland for too long. "How's it been, man? I haven't seen you in ages!" Mediochre smiled back.

"Not too bad, Jo, not too bad. I've been meaning to come see you but the job keeps getting in the way." The man addressed as Jo sat back down and gestured to the two free seats at the table. Mediochre and Charlotte sat down as Jo continued speaking.

"Yeah, whatever happened to that suspected sighting down in the Forest of Dean?" he asked. Mediochre snorted.

"Cockatrice," he said simply. Jo rolled his eyes.

"Typical. What about that one out in the Firth of Forth, better luck there?" Mediochre looked blank for a moment, and then recognition dawned on his face.

"Oh! Yes! Wyvern," he said, which seemed to impress Jo. His dark brown eyes turned to Charlotte for the first time.

"Who's this?" he asked. "New apprentice?" Mediochre rolled his eyes and spoke without looking at her.

"No. I appear to have picked up an extraphysical girl-shaped rash recently which I can't shake off," he scowled. Jo laughed.

"You should get it seen to. I know a few good doctors. Heck, I *am* a good doctor, but being still alive I think she's outside of my range of expertise. Does our rash friend have a name?"

"Charlotte," Charlotte said, unable to help but like this strange man. Jo smiled at her.

"Well I'm Doctor Joseph Carrion, Professor of Zontanecrology. Mediochre and I have known each other all my life, man and boy. Or, in his case, both at once." Charlotte tried, and failed, to work out what zontanecrology might possibly mean. Joseph Carrion was obviously used to people looking puzzled when he introduced himself, because he answered her next question before she could ask it.

"Study of the Living Dead. Zombies, Ghouls, Vampires, Ghosts, the whole lot. Often a slightly more dangerous subject than dracology, because dragons'll usually need a *reason* before they tear you apart."

He gestured now at the strange woman beside him, who had been watching their conversation silently. "This lady here is my apprentice, Dhampinella. Spelt with a D-H, pronounced with a V, don't ask me why; her parents were strange. And, as her name might suggest, she is a Sabbatical Dhampir, spelt with a D-H, pronounced with a D-H." Charlotte looked blank, and for the first time the woman named Dhampinella spoke.

"It means I'm half Vampire, and I was born on a Saturday," she explained, her voice clear and beautiful but also incredibly eerie. Charlotte couldn't help staring open-mouthed. When Dhampinella spoke, she could see her slightly elongated canines glint in the light. If Dhampinella was offended, she was an expert at hiding it.

"Dhampirs are perfectly suited to field zontanecrology," Joseph explained. "They have the ability to sense live or undead beings without looking, and are also much stronger and more agile than humans. Sabbaticals generally make even better zontanecrologists than others for some reason. The downside is that poor Dhampinella also burns far easier in sunlight than us, has a mild allergy to garlic and salt, and also a phobia of religion."

"And can be killed by a stake in the heart?" asked Charlotte weakly. Joseph raised an eyebrow.

"Most people can," he said. "Anyway, because of her natural talent, she's already learned everything I can teach her, so I mainly give her practical work-experience these days." He saw Charlotte's uncomprehending expression and grinned. "In other words, I use her to track down the Undead and any Undead-slayers around." Charlotte nodded dumbly, trying to file all this new information in amongst the thousand other new facts she'd learnt in the past hour.

Having successfully destroyed and reformed Charlotte's view of the world once more, Joseph turned his attention back to Mediochre.

"So," he said, giving Mediochre a knowing look. "I take it you have a good reason for appearing out of the blue to see me again. Let me guess. Something to do with the recent spate of dismembered dragon corpses? Someone's slaying them and smuggling the parts, right?" Mediochre nodded gravely.

"It's the SSS. Major operation, bigger than anything else recently. And I need to work out what exactly's going on, and how to stop it, but I also need to get *this* back to its mother before they find me again." He took out the gleaming dragon's egg and held it up. Joseph's eyebrows vanished temporarily into his hair.

"You nicked something back from them? You know how angry that's gonna make them." Mediochre nodded.

"It was in the Sapphire Storage depot, along with a bunch of other... dragon bits. There were a few others as well, but they'd all been too cold for too long. This one was right in the middle of the pile, sheltered from the cold, so it's not dead yet, but it's dying and I have to get it back to its cave soon." Joseph nodded seriously as Mediochre replaced the egg in its pocket. "There's a rudimentary heating charm in here with it, but now that I'm at the Uni I can get a better one – that'll keep it alive for a few days longer if we're lucky. After that I'm going back up to the mountains where I found its cave a while ago, and I'd appreciate your help in case they find me."

Joseph looked to Dhampinella, who nodded almost imperceptibly. "Mr Seth," he said, in a fair impression of Hannibal from The A-Team, "you just hired the Jo-Team."

"I love it when a plan comes together," responded Mediochre.

The pyromancer arched her back, moved her feet closer to her hands and twisted her left wrist. She couldn't remember anything after flamethrowering Seth, but she knew that she was currently in the back of her own company car with a heavy chain tied around her wrists twice, before snaking down to give her ankles the same treatment. This probably wasn't a good sign.

She managed to twist her wrist enough to release the pressure on her hand slightly – not enough to be comfortable, but enough to let the blood start circulating in her fingers again. She lay still for a moment, gathering her strength, before eventually clicking her pins-and-needles-wracked fingers. She could feel the heat as her mancy ignited the oxygen around her bound hands, but it didn't hurt her. It never did. She concentrated her power on the flame, making it grow in size and intensity. Then she rocked her body slightly a couple of times, before using the momentum to roll her off the seat and onto her back. She could feel the smoke starting to rise from the carpet of the vehicle, sense the flame spreading. Eventually the material caught, and there was an acrid smell of burning as the flames spread slowly throughout the car. They were, of course, nowhere near hot enough to melt a single metal chain.

But they would be.

Charlotte accompanied Joseph and Dhampinella to Joseph's apartment in the University while

Mediochre was off meeting some old friends of his. Joseph had offered to take her off his hands for a while, and neither Mediochre nor Charlotte objected. Joseph was laughing about his friend in a good-natured way.

"Have you heard about the time he brought down the world's biggest dragon-slaying organisation with a single blow?" he grinned.

"I, er, have, yes," replied Charlotte, thinking back to the encounter with the fake teacher and his cronies. Joseph laughed at her tone of voice.

"Sounds like he's got you into a fight already!" he said. Charlotte smiled slightly.

"Yes," she admitted. "Two, technically, although the first one wasn't so much a fight as a series of threats interspersed by running away." Joseph laughed again at that. "Is the story true?" she asked him. "'Cos he didn't seem like much of a fighter to me."

"Oh, absolutely!" replied Joseph, still grinning. "He punched the fire alarm button. They all assumed a captive dragon in the building had got loose and ran outside just as the MIPF happened to be passing."

"MIPF?" asked Charlotte, a little bewildered.

"Stands for Mantically Inclined Police Force. Cops who can do magic. Work for the MAB government."

"Oh, I see. Makes sense. What about the time he held a horde of Undead off with his teeth?"

"What *about* it?" asked Joseph.

"What happened that time?" she replied. Joseph just raised an eyebrow.

"Well, there was a horde of Undead. And he fought them off. Except his hands were full. And one of his legs was stuck."

"Oh. Right. Um."

Mediochre pressed the buzzer outside the Dean's office and waited for an answer. The door was probably unlocked and he could probably have just walked in, and she probably wouldn't have minded, but there *was* such a thing as courtesy. In matters concerning Dean Kiwi Mashuga anyway.

The door was opened by a short woman in her late forties, with hair dyed bright green for no apparent reason other than that she liked the look on people's faces the first time they saw it. She was also wearing a mango-coloured robe and mortar board, probably for the same reason, and a pair of half-moon spectacles on a garish pink ribbon. Kiwi's face broke into an impish grin when she saw Mediochre.

"I'd recognise that face anywhere," she said. "It's the only one around here I don't have to crane my neck to see." Mediochre laughed. It was true, after all.

She stepped back to let him into her office, and he smiled to himself at how little it had changed. Same woodworm-riddled desk; same overflowing in-tray; same variety of different-shaped hourglasses on the windowsill; same shocking pink carpet clashing violently with the navy-blue wallpaper; same empty mug inscribed with 'You don't have to be mad to work for me but I like it' on top of the same locked filing cabinet; same technomantic laptop whirring slightly on a corner of the desk; and quite probably the exact same unfinished paperwork strewn across everywhere else. Mediochre loved his boss's untidiness. It made him feel almost neat by comparison.

"And to what do I owe your unexpected return, Professor?" asked the Dean. "Judging by the unresolved nature of your current case, I'm assuming you haven't come to actually get back to some hard-core lecturing?" Mediochre adopted an affronted expression.

"Professor Mashuga, my lectures have never been hard-core. Not when I breeze through them so easily. Indeed, most of them are decidedly soft-core," he said. Kiwi Mashuga's eyes narrowed.

"I've told you already to call me Kiwi. It's not hard. K-I-W-I. Kiwi." Mediochre shook his head.

"Oh, no. I'm not going to stop calling you professor until you stop calling me Red," he said, with mock severity.

"Why? S'your name. Just less specifical."

"Specific, Professor." The Dean smiled again.

"So. You still haven't told me why you're here, Reddy-boy. Something to do with the case, right? You need Carrion to shoot any SSS that threaten you so you can concentrate on solving it, and you need me to give you some info, right?" Mediochre raised an eyebrow.

"Well, basically. But how do you know so much about my case all of a sudden?" Kiwi tapped her nose.

"Ah, I have my sources, Dr Red. Half the SSS secretly supply me with information on who's trying to bring them down." Mediochre laughed.

"If only that were true, what a strange place the world would suddenly become. Anyway, Prof, I need a heating charm. A *really good* heating charm. Asap. Where can I get me one of those at this time o' the day?" Kiwi thought for a moment, before replying.

"I'd go talk to Professor God if I were you." Mediochre considered this for a moment.

"OK, where can I get the best heating charm that doesn't involve talking to him?" he asked. Kiwi cackled.

"Come on," she said. "I'll do the talking for you if you want."

The burning car had now caught people's attention. Some people ran off to raise the alarm, others walked as close as they dared to see what was going on. The pyromancer focused her power and reached out to the fire with her mind, suddenly concentrating all the heat on the chains binding her hands. At the same time, she pulled and wriggled with all her strength, until eventually she was free. She quickly unchained her legs, stood up, blew the car door off its hinges and then, wrapping the fire around her like a cloak, she walked off in search of Seth.

Joseph's apartment was an awful lot tidier than Charlotte had envisaged. Everything was tidied away neatly in the open cupboard on one side, while the black single bed on the other had been made with almost unnatural precision. Perfectly parallel to the bed was a black wooden chair and table, on which was a faultlessly stacked pile of paper and a black china mug full of pens, pencils and other writing paraphernalia. Written in dripping blood-red letters on the mug was 'It's just tomato soup, honest!'. Charlotte wondered dimly if having it in the room with a vampire counted as bad taste or not.

Joseph walked straight to a small black box in the far corner of the room, and removed the lid. Charlotte couldn't see the contents from this angle, but this mattered little as Joseph removed them all, one by one.

It was a box of firearms. Charlotte, not being an expert, could not have identified any of them, and most of them were probably made by some freaky magic company that no-one knew about anyway, but they were still quite obviously the real thing. Joseph would take each one out, look at it, and then tuck it somewhere in a way that suggested he knew exactly where each one should go. Every nook and cranny of his person seemed to have a menacing black gun tucked away in it: several in his belt; a few inside his shirt; one strapped to each limb; two apparently holstered to his upper back; one in what must have been every single pocket of his coat; at least one seemingly strapped to the inside of his jeans; and she was pretty sure she saw him slip a tiny pistol of some form into his sock.

Charlotte cleared her throat faintly freaked-outedly when he finally stood up and grinned.

"Trust me, if I know Mediochre, you can never have too many firearms on one of his missions," he said jovially. Charlotte nodded slowly.

"And you acquired these firearms... how?"

"Oh, here and there," shrugged Joseph. "Most of them I bought from the same three people. It's amazing how many differently specialized guns you need in my line of work. The Undead have an annoying habit of not being killed by conventional weaponry."

Charlotte glanced at Dhampinella, but the semi-vampire was as impassive as ever. She quickly looked away. Joseph was now scribbling a note on a piece of scrap paper he'd produced from somewhere.

"Just leaving a message to say where I've gone," he said, without looking up. "The cleaning girl's a friend of mine, she'll sort it out." He suddenly straightened up, tossed the pen down on the table and walked towards the door.

"So is she the one that keeps everything neat in here?" asked Charlotte scathingly, as the pen rolled onto the floor and Joseph made no attempt to pick it up.

"She's a *good* friend," Joseph said as they left the room.

The door to Professor Your Almighty God's office opened an instant before Mediochre's hand hit it.

"Seth!" said the professor, a smile splitting his freckled face. "Lovely to see you!" Professor God was a tall, somewhat lanky man with impeccably neat short blonde hair and a permanent air of slight superiority.

"Hello, Your," grimaced Mediochre. Professor God chortled.

"Really, Seth, if you're going to shorten my full name, 'God' sounds so much better. Infinitely so."

"I'm sure it does, Your," replied Mediochre, rolling his eyes. "I'm sure it does." He stepped into the room, and Professor God saw Kiwi behind him.

"Dean! What a marvellous surprise! Did I ever tell you my theory on the etymology of Seth here's name? I believe it's all down to a deeply hidden inferiority complex. 'Mediocre', as you know, has a similar meaning to 'sub-standard', while Seth was the Ancient Egyptian's equivalent to the Devil. 'Mediochre Seth', therefore, could be taken to mean 'sub-standard devil', a term which would clearly indicate inferiority to myself, 'Your Almighty God'." Mediochre rubbed his eyes with his hand.

"I chose this name before you were even *born*, Your. Besides, it's a shade of red." The Dean seemed terribly amused by all this.

"So what does Quirinius mean then?" she asked, leaning on the wall just inside the doorway.

"Quirinius was the governor of Syria during the first census of the New Testament," rattled off Mediochre. He caught Professor God's look and smirked. "You really should read up on your namesake some time," he said, winking at Kiwi.

"Red's looking for a heating charm," the Dean interjected. "A really good heating charm." Professor God beamed suddenly.

"Why didn't you say so? I think I have just the thing! If you want heat, then heat is what I shall give you!"

At which point, in accordance with the laws of universal irony which not even Mediochre fully understood, the fire alarm sounded.

People fled in any available direction as the pyromancer walked down the corridors of St. Merlin's; they ducked into classrooms and lecture halls, sprinted down the length of the corridor and around the first available corner, or in some cases appeared to vanish into thin air or leap through solid walls. Some tried to fight her with magic, but very little of what they threw at her could get through her protective shield of flame.

In the middle of her personal inferno, the pyromancer paid them little attention. Seth wasn't among them, that much was evident. But she knew where the man would be. If he wanted his dragon egg to remain alive, he would need a heating charm. And the pyromancer knew where the heating charms were in this building. She was *good* with heating.

Mediochre, Kiwi and Professor God stepped out into the corridor as a crowd of students fled towards them from one direction and a group of security mancers pounded towards them from the other. The students arrived first, and shoved the three professors back into Professor God's office as they fought to get through the doorway themselves. Mediochre could hear the security mancers running past them as he picked himself up from the floor where he had landed.

"What's going on out there?" the Dean shouted, but Mediochre had had enough time to work out the basics of the situation for himself.

"There's an SSS agent loose in the building!" he yelled. "Probably," he added, as Kiwi Mashuga turned to him.

"Red, it always worries me when *you* start saying 'probably'," she sighed. "*Why* is there a triple-S agent loose in the building?" Mediochre closed his eyes and began tapping a rhythm on his neck with the first two fingers of his right hand.

"She was chained up in the back of the car. I was going to interrogate her once I had the heating charm. She must have... yes, she must have twisted her hands into a position where the circulation would be restored, summoned a flame, set fire to the car, and concentrated her powers on the fire until it was hot enough to make the chain links sufficiently ductile. And now she's come after me."

Mediochre ran to the door and yanked it open, with the Dean and Professor God running behind him, shouting at him to stop.

One of the security mancers shouted a warning at the raging, self-contained fireball, while another two went down on one knee and aimed weapons which resembled rifles but were attached via some form of flexible metal tubes to an oddly-shaped metal box on each one's back, vaguely reminiscent of a wasp's nest. The fireball continued to advance, so the security mancer stepped back and the other two opened fire. The weapons made a low-pitched buzzing rather than the usual boom or chatter, and a stream of tiny silver objects, too fast to make out, flew from the barrel of each towards the fireball. There was a hiss, as both streams melted and fell to the floor as a growing silvery puddle. The mancer who had shouted the warning yelled to another one standing behind him:

"Darren! Use it." The security mancer named Darren stepped forwards with his hands spread in front of him.

Mediochre noticed the sudden dryness in the air even before he opened the door. More dry than even pyromantic fire could make it so suddenly. He retched and stumbled as he emerged into the corridor.

A security mancer was standing, with the rest of his team behind him, as a large ball of white flame advanced on him. There was, inexplicably, a growing orb of floating water in each hand. The other mancers in the area were clutching their mouths or trying to cough, and a nearby water cooler was draining rapidly. Without warning, the young man pushed his hands forwards, and there were twin jets of cool, shining water flowing from his arms into the fireball. Steam filled the area with a furious hiss, but Mediochre could make out the silhouette of the pyromancer, flinching as her fire stuttered. Two armed security mancers levelled their weapons at it, but Mediochre charged forwards and yelled.

"No! Leave her!" The security mancers looked to the Dean, who snapped:

"Do as he says." The mancers lowered their weapons. Kiwi peered through the vapour and could just about make out the figure of Mediochre approaching the other one, which raised its arms...

The jets of water stopped and the steam was cleared with a flick of Darren's wrist. The pyromancer was standing in the middle of the corridor, her fire gone, staring with a look of temporary incomprehension at Mediochre, who had each of her wrists in a tight grasp. Her hands were red and unmoving.

Eventually she realised that her mancy wasn't working as there was no circulation to her fingers, and instead kicked Mediochre very hard in the shin. He yelped, let go, and stumbled backwards, and she shook some life back into her hands and raised them, and the security mancers took aim again.

And then there was a thud of metal on bone, and the pyromancer pitched forwards and hit the ground hard. Joseph Carrion stood in the corridor behind her prone form, an empty fire extinguisher in his hands.

"How did I know the alarm was your fault?" he asked, chuckling as he took Mediochre by the shoulder. "I hoped you noticed my ironic choice of weapon, by the way." Before Mediochre could reply, Charlotte came running up, with Dhampinella walking calmly beside her, somehow keeping pace without showing any apparent effort.

"Does anyone want to tell me what the hell is going on?" Charlotte panted.

"Not particularly," replied Mediochre, without turning around.

By the time everyone had been introduced, rehydrated and briefed on what had happened, the Head of Security had turned up, a grim-faced man who looked to be in his fifties.

"This wasn't just a spur-of-the-moment attack," he informed the Dean. "Someone disarmed the entire security system and overruled the usual protocol. We think the woman must have had someone already inside the building, and they must have been a very good technomancer to deactivate *everything* we had." Mediochre, who was leaning against the wall studying the man's face, cleared his throat quietly.

"Odds of 2-1 the next word to leave your mouth will be 'or'," he said. The Security Chief gave him a slightly disapproving look.

"*Or*, the SSS have had someone high-up on our faculty this whole time. You're the genius, you tell me." Mediochre looked up at the ceiling, biting his lip thoughtfully.

"*Probably* the first option. They probably wouldn't have been planning this attack so far in advance that they could get someone in here and promoted just for the purposes of allowing it. Plus, I know myself how hard it is to get into this Uni without revealing everything you may have been hiding.

"However, the attack in general makes no sense. Why go to all that trouble with the security just so a pyromancer can create a scare? You have checked that there's no-one else in here that there shouldn't be, right? Good. In that case, we can assume it was just her.

"So there is some evidence to support the fact that there was something else that the person who deactivated everything was already in place to do, which would indicate the second option. Although if that were the case, it would probably be a skilled technomancer who had got into the university staff but not for long enough to be promoted that far. A little from Column A, a little from Column B, as it were."

"Ok, then," replied the Security Chief, clearly irritated. "In that case, what do we *do*?" Mediochre looked from him to the Dean to Joseph.

"Have you interrogated the woman yet?" he asked.

"No," came the clipped response.

"Then let's get a move on."

The pyromancer was sitting, tightly handcuffed, in a bland metal chair behind a blander metal table. The room was small and nondescript, some oddly glowing squares set into the ceiling dimly lighting the featureless grey walls. The Security Chief sat opposite her, with Mediochre on his right. The Dean and Dhampinella were standing behind them, and Joseph was leaning on the wall to one side, with Charlotte standing awkwardly next to him. There was a security guard on either side of the door, and a smartly-dressed man in his sixties sat at a smaller table looking at the screen of a small hand-held device, from which a cable snaked out and connected to a metal band around the pyromancer's forehead. Joseph turned slightly and winked at Charlotte.

"We used to have a psychomancer here who could read their minds for us, but she left so we have to make do with Dr Hollis and his technomantic lie detector," he whispered. The old man gave the Security Chief the thumbs-up.

"Name," the Security Chief said, in his clipped tones. The pyromancer didn't look at him, staring instead at Mediochre, but she answered the question.

"Isobel Linda Williams. Isobel with an O."

"Truth," called out Dr Hollis. The Security Chief looked mildly disappointed.

"What were you doing in here?" he barked.

"Hunting down Seth," came the reply. Mediochre raised his eyebrows but said nothing.

"Truth."

"How did you get past our security systems?"

"What security systems?"

"The ones that were deactivated for you."

"I don't know what you're talking about." There was a pause. Then:

"Truth," said Dr Hollis, quietly. The Security Chief growled.

"Have you got someone on the faculty?"

"Me? How would *I* get someone on the faculty?"

"Answer the question."

"No."

"Truth," called out Hollis, and the Security Chief seethed with barely-concealed rage. Mediochre held up a hand before he could speak and asked:

"Does anyone in this university, and I'm not including yourself in that, work for the SSS?"

"Nope."

"Truth."

"Is there any way a member of the SSS could have known you were here?"

"Maybe. If so, it's none of my doing."

"Truth."

At this point the Security Chief slammed his hand on the table loud enough to make everyone except Mediochre and Dhampinella jump, and roared.

"What the hell is going on here?"

To which Isobel Linda Williams answered:

"If you want to know that, you're speaking to the wrong person. I only know what happened during the bits you already know about." And after a second she spoke in perfect timing with Dr Hollis:

"Truth."

Sometime later, Mediochre, Joseph, Dhampinella and Charlotte walked out through the university's front entrance. Mediochre stopped to take in the sight of the twisted black husk that had once been a car.

"Well, that was certainly a waste of several hundred pounds of company car. I hope she gets fired after she gets released," he tutted. He removed what appeared to be a small red glowstick from the depths of his body-warmer, and snapped the seal inside it. It immediately began to glow with a warm red light. "Got my heating charm at last though." Desra the mouse crawled out of the pocket he had produced the glowstick from and up onto his shoulder. Joseph reached over to stroke her affectionately.

When they got to Joseph's car, Mediochre turned to Charlotte suddenly, looking as stern as it is possible for a short fifteen-year-old boy to look.

"Now *you,* my lass, are finally going back where you came from. Your family must be worried sick." Charlotte opened her mouth to object, but couldn't think of anything to say. She didn't have to, however, because at that moment Joseph cheerfully interrupted.

"Don't worry, I've explained the situation to them already," he said jovially, waving his mobile phone in the air. "The girl can stay with us."

"WHAT?" exclaimed Mediochre, shocked. Joseph adopted what he probably thought was a suitably innocent expression.

"I thought it would be nice for you to get a chance to teach someone one-to-one. Make a nice change, wouldn't it? Besides, I like her. I let *you* keep the mouse." Mediochre raised an eyebrow.

"Joseph, you *gave* me the mouse."

"Well, yeah."

"What on earth did you *tell* her parents?" sighed Mediochre exasperatedly. Joseph smiled.

"Ah, now. That would be telling."

"Yes, Joseph," sighed Mediochre, rubbing his eyes with his hand. "Yes, it would. Congratulations on your advanced grasp of the English language. We'll make a scholar out of you yet." He opened the back door of the car and motioned to Charlotte. "I appear to be outvoted 2-1, and neither Dhampinella nor Desra seem to want a say. In you get." Charlotte's eyes widened, and for a moment she was too stunned to speak.

"Really?" she managed eventually. Mediochre merely rolled his eyes.

"Good grief, this whole scene could have stepped out of a cheesy fantasy adventure were it not for the fact that scenes are incapable of stepping anywhere due to severe deficiency in the foot department. Yes, really, now get in the car."

Joseph opted to drive rather than trust Mediochre with his car, so the dracologist took the passenger seat instead. That left Charlotte alone in the back with Dhampinella, an arrangement that she wasn't entirely happy about. The tall silent Dhampir seemed to radiate an aura of unease, so that one always felt uncomfortable when one got too close to her. Nevertheless, Charlotte decided to try and engage her in conversation, in the hope that this might break the spell, or whatever it was.

"So, how did you become Joseph's apprentice then?" she asked as cheerfully as she could. Dhampinella did not turn her head to look at her when she answered.

"He took me on after I helped him catch my father's killer." Charlotte found herself lost for words.

"O...K..." she eventually managed.

"If it helps your emotional confusion, my father was a particularly nasty person, even by Vampire standards," explained Dhampinella, in the same emotionless monotone. Charlotte shuffled slightly in her seat.

"Have... have you any other family?" she asked, unable to curb her own curiosity. Dhampinella did not seem offended when she answered, however.

"My mother disowned my family and fled when I was quite young. I have a fully Vampire half-sister from my father's previous marriage. We speak little."

It struck Charlotte that perhaps the reason Dhampinella's speech held so little emotion was that Vampires showed emotion in a completely different way. She decided it would be simpler to just stop making any attempts at conversation.

Meanwhile, in the front of the car, Mediochre and Joseph were having a different conversation.

"So why do you think the Triple-S have suddenly diversified so heavily into dragon parts?" asked Joseph in hushed tones. Mediochre looked grim.

"I can think of several reasons, none of which are *particularly* probable. Mostly they boil down to either someone paying them a lot to gather as many as possible or someone high-up in the syndicate wanting to attract attention."

"The attention of you, for example?" asked Joseph. "You are the world's leading figure on pro-dragon campaigning."

"Possibly," replied Mediochre. "And *that* would introduce a whole new set of questions. I need to know some more of the variables before I can work this one out."

"And that's why we're visiting Melinda?" said Joseph, somewhere between a statement and a question.

"That," Mediochre confirmed, "is why we're visiting Melz."

Melinda Quinn, as Joseph explained to Charlotte, was one of Mediochre's oldest friends. They had been students at St Merlin's together at least once, and she had even once served as his apprentice before she decided she wasn't cut out for field Dracology. As far as Joseph was concerned, Melinda was the only human being in the universe who knew more about Mediochre than he did. He even sometimes speculated that she knew more about Mediochre than Mediochre did.

Melinda's house was remarkably ordinary-looking from the outside. After the grandeur of St Merlin's, Charlotte had been half-expecting a mansion or something, but it was just a house with slightly-crumbling whitewashed brick walls and a dull brown front door. One thing that was unusual about it, though, was that the door unlocked and opened itself when Mediochre set foot in the driveway.

"Nice to see the old place still recognises me," Mediochre said, somewhat enigmatically.

Inside, the house also looked fairly normal. Cream-coloured carpet in the hall, stairs leading up to a second floor, pictures of family members hanging on the walls. Nothing remarkable, nothing magic. The door to the living room didn't even open on its own; Mediochre had to turn the handle. All a bit of an anticlimax, really. Inside the living room, a grey-haired old woman in a pink cardigan and prim grey skirt sat in a dark brown armchair, with a small wooden table to her left, on which was a half-empty teacup. Apart from that, there wasn't much to speak of in the room except an old electric fire and a few more, identical armchairs. The woman did not turn to greet them, or even recognise that they had entered the room.

Smiling, Mediochre slowly approached the old woman, very gently lifting her right hand and turning it palm-upwards. He began to lightly press or rub various parts of the woman's hand, as if he was performing sign language using one of his own hands and one of hers. When he had finished the woman smiled and, weakly grasping the hand in her own, turned as if to look Mediochre in the eye.

Charlotte gasped as she saw the woman's face. The eyes were completely white, devoid entirely of both iris and pupil. Joseph leaned towards Charlotte and whispered in her ear.

"Melinda's both deaf and blind. Mediochre can now only communicate to her via touch. It's a tragic shame, really, because if she could see even a little she would be one of the most renowned artists in the world." He straightened up. "I'll go put the kettle on," he called to Mediochre as he left through a door at the far end of the room.

Charlotte was suddenly aware that she needed to visit the bathroom, and that she couldn't speak to the owner of the house and Mediochre and Joseph were both otherwise engaged. She turned to Dhampinella who had taken up a position by the door and was standing impassively.

"Er... do you know where the bathroom is in this house?" she asked nervously. Dhampinella looked at her in a disconcerting way.

"Upstairs," she said, and went back to standing impassively.

"Er... thank you," replied Charlotte uneasily, as she left the room.

As she left the bathroom, Charlotte was surprised to find another girl leaning against the wall opposite. Charlotte estimated the girl was about the same age as her, although sat first glance she looked older, really more of a young woman than a girl. Only her lack of height gave her away. There was a sort of streetwise nonchalance to the way she was leaning casually against the wall, her impressive figure clad in a scarlet t-shirt and black jeans with a thick black belt around her waist, her face framed by her long hair which was almost as red as the shirt.

"Hey," said the girl by way of greeting, her eyes briefly flicking down and back up, taking Charlotte in.

"Um.... hey," replied Charlotte, somewhat self-consciously. The girl smiled at that, and straightened up.

"I take it you're with MQ 'Ochre. New apprentice? I bet that'll shake up the MABGov a bit."

"Uh... no," replied Charlotte, "Not exactly. I'm... actually, I'm not really sure what I am. I just seem to have been, sort of, brought along for the ride." That made the strange girl laugh, a bizarrely musical sound. She put an arm around Charlotte's shoulders and began to lead her towards a door at the end of the corridor.

"Yeah, 'Ochre does that," she said as they walked. "He's a weird guy. But *good* weird. Mostly."

"Um... sorry, who *are* you?" asked Charlotte hesitantly.

"You say 'um' a lot, dontcha?" smiled the girl, imitating Charlotte's accent.

"Uh...." replied Charlotte. The girl laughed before she could think up an answer.

"Rowan," she said as she pushed open the door. "Rowan Berry. My great-aunt's downstairs talking with Mediochre." It took Charlotte a second to get the joke, and then she smiled.

"I'm Charlotte," she said. "Where are we going, exactly?" Rowan smiled mysteriously.

"I want to show you something. It might help you understand things better."

"Mediochre," said Melinda in a hoarse whisper. "It's nice to feel your touch again."

It's always nice to see you, Melz, signed Mediochre on her hand. A smile broke across Melinda's creased face.

"Who did you bring with you this time?" she asked.

Joseph. Dhampinella. A new girl named Charlotte. Melinda raised her eyebrows.

"A new apprentice?"

No. Just a schoolgirl whom Joseph took along. I think he just wants to annoy me. She's a decent enough kid, fairly bright, but I don't think she's dracologist material.

"Ah," said Melinda, knowingly. "You should give her a chance. She may surprise you yet. It would do you good to get another one after all these years."

I know. Everyone keeps saying that. Melinda patted his hand.

"They're right you know. But I'm sure you didn't come here to discuss apprentices. You want to speak to Rowan?"

Yes. I need some information about a few things so I can stop the systematic destruction of the dragon species as we know it. At that, Melinda looked suddenly sad.

"Oh dear. Not again."

I'm afraid so. Worse this time.

"How long since the last time now?"

About 350 years.

"Really? Seems less. Aged any?"
Couple of months. Still 15. You?
"I've almost reached 100."

Charlotte climbed down a ladder Rowan had revealed beneath a trap door in her great-aunt's room. When she got to the bottom she turned around and gasped. Rowan was leaning against the wall, smiling, and all throughout the huge room, the nearest one only a few feet away, were hundreds of thin partition-like boards, on which were hung thousands of pictures.

Pictures that moved. Charlotte stepped forwards to touch the nearest one. It felt like ordinary wood; but on the surface, playing on a loop, a magnificent dark brown stag leapt over a fallen tree, over and over and over. Charlotte was lost for words.

"Great-aunt Melz used to be 'Ochre's apprentice," explained Rowan, "but she soon discovered that her talent for dracology was far surpassed by her talent for iconomancy – the magic of images. In this room is every work she's ever created: some from life, some from imagination; some unmoving, some that play a single action over and over again, some that show an hour or more's movement on a continuous loop."

Charlotte ran her gaze over the nearby images, some that looked like impressionist paintings, and some that looked so realistic she felt the urge to reach out and touch them.

"Can you do this stuff too?" she asked, incredulously. By way of answer, Rowan ran her fingers through a lock of her brilliantly red hair. Instantly, the colour dimmed to a more normal shade of brownish-ginger. She twisted the lock in her fingers and it reverted back to the bolder red it had been before.

"I'm nowhere near as good as her, but I'm learning," she said. "Mel's so good that if she concentrates, she can actually see again by mantically forcing an image of what's around her into her own brain. Don't ask me how that works. Anyway, the ones I wanted to show you are all over here."

Charlotte let herself be led through the labyrinth of images until they reached one particular board. She looked at the first moving image. It showed two college-age guys playing a rather intense game of table-tennis. There wasn't any sound, but you could tell from their faces that they were both laughing. There was a younger boy behind them playing a fast piano piece, probably a ragtime solo from the way he was moving. Charlotte peered closer at the man on the left. It was Joseph. Younger and dressed differently, but unmistakably Joseph.

And then the pianist turned around and said something to him, without stopping his playing. It was Mediochre.

Charlotte looked across at another picture on the right-hand side of the board. This one showed a woman in a hospital bed holding a tiny baby in her arms. On one side of the bed was an incredibly proud-looking man, stroking the baby's face gently. On the other side of the bed, grinning, his hand on the woman's shoulder, was Mediochre.

Charlotte glanced across at another image on a subsequent board. A despairing Mediochre, running a hand through his hair as he looked around at a vast expanse of churned-up mud dotted with poppies. This time he looked a little older, as if his body hadn't finished de-aging yet.

"Rowan... how long have Mediochre and Melinda known each other?" she asked, as her eyes flicked across various pictures of various differently-aged Mediochres, one on a rural farm, one watching a group of protesting miners from the sidelines, one spoon-feeding a scarily skinny African child, one watching the departure of *the HMS Titanic* of all things, one apparently running across a rooftop in what looked like Victorian London...

"Ever since she became his apprentice, some point around the 17th Century I think," said Rowan, quietly. "They were involved in the same accident that made them basically immortal, but Melz wasn't hit so bad. She kept on aging, it just slowed it down gradually, until now she's a blind, deaf 100-year-old but she still won't die. After that, Mediochre's been scared to take on another apprentice because he doesn't want to put anyone else through that."

"So... when you say she's your great-aunt...?" inquired Charlotte. Rowan nodded.

"I may have missed out a few greats," she said. There was silence for a while.

"Rowan?" asked Charlotte. "Do you know what the magical accident they were in actually involved?" For a moment Rowan looked as if she was about to answer, but then another voice cut through the room before she could.

"If she does," announced Mediochre, walking around the corner of a nearby board, "she's not permitted to tell you."

"Hey MQ," said Rowan, apparently unfazed. She reached out with her arm until her fingertips brushed lightly against his wrist. Desra crawled out of his sleeve and scampered up Rowan's arm. "S'up D," she said fondly, stroking the tiny rodent on her shoulder.

Mediochre straightened the picture of him with the new mother, gave it an appraising look for a moment, briefly adjusted the angle of his hat, and turned to face the girls.

"So," he said, fishing his wallet from one of his pockets. "Rowan. Any info on the SSS and/or the recent spate of dragon deaths?" Rowan looked thoughtful.

"Well, there's a couple of rumours that the Triple-S are going out of business, although no-one seems to be sure why. And Foynitcha Dave says he has it on good authority that they were behind that bunch of New York kidnappings that everyone says must have been done mantically."

"Kidnapping humans?" mused Mediochre. "That's definitely not the normal Triple-S way." Rowan shrugged.

"As for these dragon deaths, the only thing I got on that is a crazy story that it's some big-shot dragon slayer from years ago back from the dead." Mediochre nodded thoughtfully.

"That's... possible. Interesting certainly. I may need Joseph's help on that one. Thanks." He removed some cash from his wallet, folded it into a paper aeroplane and tossed it to Rowan. "Keep me posted on anything else relevant that comes up. And possibly also anything completely irrelevant but nevertheless interesting."

Rowan stopped stroking Desra, allowed her to scurry back down her arm to Mediochre's waiting hand, and gave a mock salute. Then she winked at Charlotte and disappeared around a board of paintings.

"Well," said Mediochre. "Unless Joseph's got bored of you already, I deduce that it looks like you're a-coming with us. We're absconding this city tomorrow morning, but I'm sure I have a spare room somewhere you can spend the night, provided you don't put my electricity bill through the roof or attempt to host a rave." He stopped, considering. "Or, you know, a paintball session or a nuclear war or anything else that would trash the place."

"I think I get the point," sighed Charlotte, rolling her eyes.

As it turned out, Mediochre did have a room to spare. In fact, from the look of things, he had several. His house was *huge*.

"I thought you said dracology didn't pay well?" asked Charlotte accusingly.

"It doesn't," replied Mediochre. "But I refuse to sell the house. This house has been in my family for generations." He furrowed his brow slightly. "Well, technically I was the first member of my family to own it. But it's still been in the family for the *equivalent* of generations."

"Doesn't anyone get suspicious that this house has been registered in the same person's name for so long?" asked Charlotte. Mediochre rolled his eyes.

"Of course not. None of the Mantically Unaware know this place exists. Like the university, it's been enchanted so that it can't be noticed except by a mancer or someone who's been shown it by someone who knows it's there already. Don't ask me how it works; I do dragons, not enchantments."

The house was classical in its architecture, and Charlotte had to remind herself that for all she knew that had been considered cutting-edge design when Mediochre was younger. Or older. Whatever. The wooden door had two elaborate coats of arms carved into it: one showing a pair of dragons coiled around a crown with the motto 'VIM PROMOVET DRACONIS', and one showing a longsword with a crown of thorns around the hilt and the motto 'UBI CARITAS ET AMOR DEUS IBI EST'.

"That's the Royal Society for Dracology's crest and Mediochre's Bloodline Crest," said Joseph as they approached. "With everyone in the Knower community choosing their own name, the Crest is the only way of identifying who's related to who."

"Whom," corrected Mediochre without turning around, as he unlocked the door and opened it. Charlotte followed him inside and felt her eyebrows rise automatically. There was no form of corridor or entrance hall. The door opened straight onto some sort of old-fashioned sitting room with gothic-looking leather armchairs, a solid oak table at one end, a magnificent grand piano, an iron fireplace flanked by two stone dragons, and an assortment of pictures on the wall of the non-moving kind. These ranged from a large portrait of Mediochre in highland regalia which hung above the fireplace to a painting of a huge navy-blue dragon on a pile of gold to a replica (presumably) of the Monarch of the Glen to, for no apparent reason, an incredibly detailed close-up of a goldfish. Mediochre turned in the middle of it, his arms outstretched, a slightly-manic grin on his face. "Well?" he asked. "What do you think?"

"Um..." was about all Charlotte could manage, which sent both Mediochre and Joseph into fits of laughter. Dhampinella, as usual, merely stood impassively beside her tutor.

"Don't worry," Joseph reassured her, clapping her on the shoulder. "He did it up like this deliberately because he found it amusing to watch people's expressions upon entering. The rest of the place isn't nearly so, er, decorated."

"Right..." said Charlotte, casting her eyes around the room. Joseph ushered her over to the door into the hallway which, as it turned out, was indeed much more normal.

Mediochre stepped into his study and used Chips to turn on the light. He surveyed the room for a few moments, frowning, and then picked up a book from the top of one of the many piles of clutter. The *Ars Draconis.*

"That's not where you should be," he muttered. "I hope the caretaker hasn't been messing around in here again. Mind you, if it wasn't him that'd mean someone without the authority to get through the security measures has got in, so..." as he tailed off, the heavy leather-bound book slipped from his grasp and landed on his foot. "*Ars,*" he muttered, bending to pick it up again. He slung the book onto another pile of clutter indiscernible from the original pile of clutter, moved to a clutter-ridden desk, swept some clutter aside, and took out the dragon's egg with its heating charm. Desra crawled up onto his hat and curled up, without Mediochre apparently noticing. A salamander-like creature in a glass case pressed itself against the glass, trying to see the source of heat. Mediochre brushed his fringe from his eyes, reached out for a microscope and placed the egg very carefully under a lamp.

"Let's see exactly what you are, shall we?" he said quietly.

Joseph Carrion removed his coat and threw it in the general direction of a chair. Most of the weapons concealed on his person he dumped at the side of his bed along with his clothes, although one particular one he kept in the waistband of his underwear as he got into bed. Just in case. He checked a few things on his IMP, before dropping it onto the bedside table.

He was worried. There seemed to be something wrong with Mediochre, but not even he could work out what, and he'd known the man since birth. He also had a sneaking suspicion that the only reason why they were waiting until the morning to set off was that Mediochre was trying to put it off. He knew something about this case that he wasn't telling anyone. And that was *always* a bad sign.

Joseph sighed softly, and tried to get some sleep. If he knew Mediochre, which he did, then they were in for a very tiring adventure.

Charlotte sat on the bed and looked around. Joseph had been right, the room looked deceptively normal. Cream wallpaper, beige carpet; it could easily have been a hotel room except for a small moving picture on the opposite wall of a brownish-red dragon flying through the night sky.

It was hard to believe that this fairly boring room could be part of the same world as houses that couldn't be noticed; agencies that smuggled illegal dragon parts; and humans that couldn't age and could recover from third-degree burns in seconds. It was also hard to believe that a few hours ago she had been just another bored schoolgirl in a country she didn't like.

It was odd, really. This new world was responsible for almost running her over with a truck, having her held at gunpoint, and nearly fricasseeing her alive, but if she had the choice she didn't think she'd ever want to go back to her old one.

How had she even ended up here? It all seemed to have happened so fast, she wasn't even sure herself.

Dhampinella rejected the idea of sleeping in the bed provided in favour of lying full-length on a wooden bench, still fully clothed, her hands folded neatly on her stomach. That might have seemed a little odd to a normal person, but then, her father had slept at night in his own coffin.

Her reddish hair fell across her face as she closed her eyes. She looked exactly like a corpse – even the rising and falling of her chest as she breathed slowed dramatically and became less obvious. She made no sound or movement as she slept in the cold, dark room. Dhampinella always slept like this. It reminded her of her youth. Not even Joseph knew why.

Mediochre sat on the piano stool in his sitting room, facing parallel to the piano beside him, with his legs crossed and a ponderous, brooding expression behind the hair that had fallen over his face. His head was leaning on the fist of one hand, while the other arm was stretched out at right angles to his body, the fingers dancing over the piano keys, playing *Fur Elise* repeatedly; an impressive feat with only one hand. How long he had been like this it was hard to tell. Perhaps the whole night. Nobody in the world knew whether Mediochre Q Seth actually needed sleep. There were a lot of things that nobody in the world knew about Mediochre Q Seth.

Nobody in a position to tell anyone, anyway.

Certainly nobody stupid enough to do so against his will.

His hand kept dancing across the piano and his brain kept calculating, relentlessly, throughout the night.

Joseph had awoken shortly before dawn, and was now standing, all firearms replaced in their correct positions, with a glass pressed against the wall and his ear pressed to the glass. He checked his watch and waited expectantly.

Then he heard it: the strange cross between a scream and a whimper. The sound of someone waking up and realising that they've just spent the past night in the house of a complete stranger with abilities that directly contradict everything they previously thought they knew about science.

Joseph smiled. He had a feeling life would be much more entertaining with this kid around to question everything.

Charlotte sat up, groaned, and checked once more that she was awake and this hadn't all been a bizarre dream. She was still wearing her school uniform, and her schoolbag was lying against the side of the bed. How could all this have happened? She had no idea what on Earth she'd thought she'd been doing yesterday. She wondered whether this was what it felt like to be in shock.

Slowly, as if worried the weight of all the crazy memories might make her head come off, she made her way downstairs and into Mediochre's sitting room.

Mediochre was sitting in a high-backed leather chair, reading a large leather-bound book. The hand that he wasn't using to turn the pages was holding a whisky glass by its base, swirling the contents gently. The effect was slightly spoiled by the fact that on the table in front of him was not a whisky decanter but a bottle of lemonade and a carton of pressed apple juice.

"I don't drink alcohol as a rule," he said. "It does terrible things to the 15-year-old liver. But a mix of apple and lemonade is much more refreshing anyway." Only then did he look up at Charlotte. "You're awake, I see."

"Um... yes," replied Charlotte.

"And suffering from delayed mild shock, which is only to be expected," continued Mediochre. "Have some toast. It probably won't help, but at least you won't be in shock *and* hungry at the same time, which I imagine would suck." He gestured to the plate beside the lemonade bottle.

At that moment, Joseph came sliding side-saddle down the banister of the staircase, careered past Charlotte and landed in a nonchalant position in the chair beside Mediochre.

"Morning all," he said cheerfully. Mediochre rolled his eyes.

"You woke Desra up," he replied, as a tiny nose appeared from one of his pockets and sniffed the air.

"Well, that makes five of us then," smiled Joseph, looking at a point somewhere to the left of Charlotte, who turned to see Dhampinella standing beside her, viewing her impassively. She flinched and stepped backwards. Dhampinella did not respond.

"Since when have you been there?" Charlotte asked incredulously. Dhampinella gave an odd sort of half-shrug.

"Sixish."

Mediochre suddenly closed his book with a sharp thump and placed it carefully beside his chair.

"That was a predictable twist," he sighed. "They always are nowadays." He drained his glass and set it down on the table in front of him, before steepling his fingers. "Anyway, the situation may be graver than I thought. Our dragon egg isn't just any old dragon's egg – it's the egg of what appears to be the only surviving case of a dragon with TST."

"Which is...?" Charlotte prompted, gesturing for him to continue.

"Which is an abbreviation of Trans-Species Telepathy," replied Mediochre. "A very rare trait only ever seen in dragons, which almost completely died out some time ago. Dragons have a distinctly weird biology, and one of the apparently impossible things about it is that genetic traits such as this can actually disappear completely from the gene pool – not even unaffected carriers remain. The science behind it is incredibly complex and totally beyond the capacity of a non-mantically-aware scientist, but the fact remains: everyone thought this trait no longer existed. Now it turns out that there are two carriers of it left in the universe. The parent dragon –"

"And our egg," finished Joseph, all traces of playfulness gone from his expression. Mediochre nodded.

"I think I'm gonna call it Glint," he added. "It looks like a Glint."

"So... waitaminute," said Joseph, raising a hand and furrowing his brow. "Do the Triple-S know about this?"

"Almost definitely," replied Mediochre. "They let the others die because they thought they'd make more money from selling them as pretty decorations than as potential pets – understandably enough, since it's easier to sell a tiger pelt than a tiger. But now they've been told that the parent had TST – probably by their pet slayer when they sent him in to kill her - and have realised the potential outcome of that: that Glint could be worth enough to buy every member of the syndicate a comfortable retirement."

"So when they were trying to steal it from you..." said Joseph. Mediochre nodded again.

"They didn't want to kill it before I took it back. They wanted to sell it before it died. Or before I presented it to the scientific community."

Silence descended like a blanket. Joseph put his hand on the back of his neck and blew out his cheeks thoughtfully. Dhampinella stood impassively, but perhaps in a slightly more sombre way than usual. Charlotte stood awkwardly, not entirely sure what to do. Mediochre stroked Desra quietly. Then Joseph spoke.

"So... what are we going to do with it? *Should* we take it to the scientific community?" Mediochre stood up.

"Nope. We're taking it back to its mother. Quite apart from not wanting to split up a family, it's not what the SSS will expect me to do. And I've always found that there's a certain boyish glee involved in putting people you don't like on the back foot, haven't you?" There was just a hint of tightening around the corners of Mediochre's mouth – not quite an immature grin, but an immature grin waiting to happen.

"But won't they have someone watching to see where you go next?" asked Dhampinella, making Charlotte jump away from her involuntarily.

"Nope," replied Mediochre, finally breaking into the grin he'd been threatening to. "Cos they'll be trying to fourth-guess me, having worked out already that I'm too smart for first-, second-, or third-guessing. Which means they won't be stupid enough to just put me under surveillance since if they did I'd just trick them."

He must have caught Charlotte's expression, because he sighed slightly in a light-hearted fashion.

"Trust me on this one."

Mediochre went upstairs to collect the egg, and since he didn't seem to mind Charlotte decided to follow him. He didn't look at her as he opened the door and stepped inside.

Charlotte gasped as she took in the room. Part laboratory, part study and part loft, it was full of various piles of books, boxes and bizarre paraphernalia. The egg and its heating charm were set in a special stand on what was probably a desk, although the actual surface of it could not be seen. Containers and jars of unidentified plants and minerals littered the desk, along with a microscope, a rack of sealed test tubes containing some form of gaseous substance, a huge fossilised claw and a curious lizard-type being in a glass case with some soil, a bowl of water, a few weeds and another of the glow-stick-shaped heating charms. Whatever the creature was, its scales were the same colour as most of Mediochre's clothing.

"*Salamandris Mantico*," said Mediochre, looking up at her and following her gaze. "Literally 'Magical Salamander', although it's actually a lizard. They exist in a symbiotic relationship with dragons, absorbing energy from the heat given off by the dragon's body and eating any ticks the dragon may get infested with. Salamandris hide is also the most flame-retardant naturally-occurring material, probably because they live in constant threat from being lightly toasted when their dragon friends attack intruders. You may have noticed the remarkable lack of burn marks on my clothes despite having had a mad pyromancer try to flame-grill me."

At this, he spread his arms wide and looked down at his own body-warmer. Charlotte noticed that Mediochre seemed much more amicable when he was talking about his specialist subject. She also had to admit that it was all rather fascinating; certainly better than the biology they taught her at school.

Mediochre scooped the egg and the heating charm into one of his pockets, turned off the lights with a flick of his IMP and dragged Charlotte gently but firmly out of his study. As they were going back downstairs and out to Joseph's waiting car, Charlotte inquired politely about how the 'apprentice' system everyone kept talking about worked. Mediochre looked slightly uncomfortable, but told her anyway.

"It's one of the few times it's legal for a Knower to reveal the existence of mancy to an Ignorant. Basically, a professional from a mantically-based job, such as dracology or zontanecrology, chooses a specific person, either Mantically-Aware of Mantically-Unaware, whom they believe has the necessary qualities to become a professional in said subject themselves, and he or she teaches this person everything they know, one-to-one, and is effectively responsible for their future career in this subject. Most people choose an apprentice as soon as they become an expert at their job, but the last apprentice I has was Melz, and that was a heck of a long time ago. I'm not sure if I really should take on another."

"Can't you work out whether it'd be a good idea or not with your crazy probability power?" Charlotte pointed out. Mediochre shook his head.

"All I can work out is the probable consequences, not whether it's right or not."

"What's the difference?" asked Charlotte, raising an eyebrow.

"Well," replied Mediochre. "Take Romeo and Juliet. You haven't read it, but I assume you know the basic storyline?"

"Um... yes," replied Charlotte, wondering exactly what Mediochre meant when he said 'basic'.

"Right," went on Mediochre, without apparently noticing her tone. "Say someone had stopped Mercutio challenging Tybalt. Knocked him on the back of the head and dragged him off home or something, I don't know. Then, by my calculations, which are never wrong by the way, Mercutio, Tybalt, Paris, Romeo, Juliet and Lady Montague would not have died. However, the feud would have continued for several more years, resulting in the violent deaths of about 37 people before Prince Escalus finally managed to stop it.

Which of those options is the right one?" Charlotte frowned slightly, thinking.

"The one that resulted in fewest deaths I suppose," she said uncertainly.

"Right," replied Mediochre. "That's what most people say. Except that Juliet was a child. She was thirteen years old. And Romeo, Mercutio and Tybalt were probably only in their late teens at most. All the people who would have died otherwise were violent, battle-loving, middle-aged men. They didn't deserve to die, obviously, but at least they had already made their choice." There was silence for a while as they arrived at Joseph's car and got in and Charlotte reflected on what Mediochre had said. After a while, she gave up and instead asked:

"So... do you look this deeply into *everything* you read?" Mediochre looked around from his seat in the front of the car.

"When you've been alive as long as I have, you have to find new ways of entertaining yourself," he replied.

Mediochre's plan was that they should leave the city in Joseph's car, and then meet up with an old contact of Mediochre's who would drive them to the Cairngorms, whereupon they would get out and walk. Meanwhile, another old contact of Mediochre's would provide a decoy by doubling back in Joseph's now-abandoned car and head back into the city. Mediochre was currently on the phone to some *other* other old contacts, to 'distract the Triple-S's distractions and insure against their insurances' as he put it. The man had more contacts than an optician for giant spiders.

"And you're *sure* this'll be enough to throw 'em?" queried Joseph when they stopped at some traffic lights, one hand subconsciously stroking the gun in his belt. Mediochre gave him a mock withering look.

"I *did* just spend all night at the piano working out their next moves you know," he smiled.

"Um... piano?" repeated Charlotte, confusedly. Mediochre shrugged.

"It helps me concentrate. My skills with probability work best when playing the piano, and worst when running like the blazes from a murderous psychopath."

"He tested this by scientific experiment," added Joseph. "Repeatedly."

Charlotte had to admit after half an hour of driving that she'd never envisaged outwitting a diabolical smuggling ring as being this easy. Or this boring. For want of anything else to do, she checked her phone.

There was nothing. That was odd. She'd been missing now for over twelve hours and no-one had sent her so much as a 'where are you?' text message. How *had* Joseph explained her disappearance? It must have been pretty convincing not to have aroused suspicion by now.

Dhampinella suddenly stiffened, her glittering green eyes flicking around the interior of the car at superhuman speeds.

"Joseph," she said quietly, causing Charlotte to shiver involuntarily. Mediochre and Joseph both looked around anxiously, neither apparently caring that Joseph was supposed to be keeping his eyes on the road.

"What is it?" asked Mediochre. Dhampinella's eyes did not cease their movement.

"There was another living thing in this car," said Dhampinella, just the slightest traces of what sounded like fear starting to creep into her eerily beautiful voice.

"What?" exclaimed both Charlotte and Mediochre. Dhampinella finally stopped glancing around , but still seemed distressed.

"Just for a moment," she explained. "The tiniest fraction of a second. But it was definitely there." Joseph breathed out heavily.

"If this was anyone but you, I'd be asking if you were sure," he said. He turned his gaze to Mediochre.

"Medi, how's that even possible? How can someone appear in our car for just an instant? Teleportation or something?" Mediochre looked thoughtful for a moment, then twisted his fingers through his fringe in agitation.

"Nope," he said. "Tempomancy. Someone stopped time, or at least slowed it down almost infinitely, for long enough to get in and then leave. Almost certainly the same tempomancer that was with the SSS members who came after Glint in the school. Which logically means –"

"That the Triple-S now know where we are," finished the other three. Mediochre removed Glint the egg from his pocket, and examined it.

"The thing that *really* doesn't make sense, though, is that he-slash-she came in here and didn't bother to steal Glint. So what exactly are they trying to do?"

"Get our attention?" suggested Joseph. Mediochre considered.

"No reason why they would want to. Unless we've had their motives wrong from the start. In which case, what do *they* need *our* attention for?" There was a brief period of thoughtful silence, before Mediochre said, "Joseph, are you aware that the road curved off to the left back there and we're currently driving through a field?"

As Joseph yelped and tried to reverse back onto the road, Charlotte realised that she was still holding her phone. She looked down at it, and gasped quietly. The tempomancer hadn't just stopped time for long enough to get in and out of the car. He'd also had time to type a message on Charlotte's phone:

The others will not trust us. Please do not tell anyone about us. Speak to Danny. There is more at stake than you know. Do not show anyone this message.

Charlotte hesitated for a moment or two, then deleted the message and replaced the phone in her pocket.

*

Mr Antler had given up watching the door when he was waiting for the tempomancer to arrive, because the man seemed to think it terribly amusing to merely appear in front of him, apparently out of thin air. He sat in his office in the back-up facility he'd had to move all his operations to after the Sapphire Storage Facility had its cover blown. The large blond head of the British branch of the SSS sincerely hoped it didn't happen again; he was in a lot of trouble over that one.

He brushed some non-existent dust from his spotless dinner suit and went back to skimming the notes on the various final operations the SSS was performing before its retirement. After a while, he realised that the voice in his head reading them aloud was not actually in his head. He turned.

The tempomancer was surveying the notes over his shoulder, mumbling them aloud in a perfect impression of Mr Antler's own voice. When he noticed Antler had noticed him he smiled and stopped. The man had a smile like a cat that was just about to dismember its prey.

"There were some problems in the acquiring of the actual egg, sir," the tempomancer said in his accentless, emotionless voice. "But I do know where they are headed and the perfect place to intercept them." He smiled and stepped backwards, his body language inviting Antler to ask for the location. Antler scowled. He had been glad to have the tempomancer on his side at first; the man had some invaluable skills after all. But lately he was beginning to annoy Antler. It wasn't that the tempomancer seemed to think he was more important than anyone else; it was that he seemed to *know* he was more important than anyone else, but he refused to explain why.

"Very well," said Antler through gritted teeth. "We shall call back all our back-ups and send some forces out to this 'perfect interception place'."

"Ah, yes, another thing," said the tempomancer, his smile unwavering. "He seems to have been a step ahead of us on the back-up front."

Jonah and Oscar Charlson, better known as the Bomb Brothers, completed the finishing touches to their tempomantic incendiary device. They didn't know or care why they had been commissioned to construct it, merely that their clients wanted this train station out of operation and out of operation it would therefore be. You could always rely on the Bomb Brothers.

Jonah stood up inspected their work, and then jerked his thumb over his shoulder.

"C'mon Oscar. We're done here, let's roll." He turned to leave, and found his path blocked by an amicable-looking white-haired man in a brown suit and tie, carrying an umbrella in the crook of an elbow.

"What the-?" spluttered Oscar as Jonah yelped with surprise. "Who the hell are you?" he yelled in shock when he saw the man. "What the hell are you doing down here?" The man smiled.

"Forthan Forth, at your service," he said politely. "And I could ask you the same question." Jonah and Oscar looked at each other nervously. Neither of them were violent men, once you learnt to ignore the whole explosive-creation side of things.

"Look buddy," said Jonah. "We don't want anyone to get hurt..." The man smiled again.

"In that case," he said respectfully, "I suspect you'll be wanting to dismantle your bomb and come with me." And with that he tugged the handle of his umbrella and produced a gleaming katana.

Robert Zoderick Carapanalina, known to his good friends as Bob-Zod, walked calmly towards the group of gunpeople hidden behind a clump of bushes at the side of the road.

"You're wasting your time," he called once he got in range. "He's not coming this way." The gunpeople all simultaneously turned, yelled a serious of confused exclamations, and took aim. Only then did they realise that they were crouched in front of a lake, and Bob-Zod was walking on the water.

Before anyone could react, Bob-Zod raised both hands in a dramatic gesture and a huge wave sprang up and washed the group into the road.

A man and a woman stood in the street, trying to look casual, looking out for anyone heading towards St Merlin's University. Neither had met the other before they were put on this mission, and both were silent as they waited. They thought nothing of it when they heard footsteps behind them; after all it was the *other* direction they'd been told Mediochre might be coming from. They *did* however notice when their heads were sharply banged together from behind.

"That was easy," remarked Professor God as the two SSS agents collapsed with a series of muffled curses and he was able to toss a technomantic holding net over them. "I don't know why Seth sounded so unhappy to be asking me to do it for him."

Beth Diamond saw the thug looking at her and smiled. She tossed her long platinum-blonde hair back and winked at him. She could see the obvious struggle in the thug's mind – should he guard the building like he'd been paid to or should he go speak to the pretty woman who was now approaching a side alley and could soon be gone?

Eventually he apparently decided that if it was all that important, the SSS people would have paid more than one guy to guard the stupid building, so he set of after the alley entrance. He found Beth leaning against the wall just inside and grinned. Beth grinned back, before using her mancy to suck the heat from the alley. The thug gave her a look of dumb surprise, and she rolled her eyes and stamped on his feet, freezing them to the ground with a thick covering of ice, before walking away.

"Would've kept guarding the building if I were you," she called over her shoulder as she removed her mobile and dialled the MIPF.

"So you're telling me," said Antler, his eyes narrowing, "that every one of our back-up operations has been thwarted, several of our valued operatives have been captured and arrested, and no-one thought to inform me of this?" The tempomancer made a non-committal gesture. Antler curled his massive hand into a fist. "We'll just have to bring out the big guns then. Although we might want to stall them first with some slightly lesser guns." He smiled cruelly.

*

It was in a state of paranoid agitation that Joseph pulled into the secluded field and got out of the car. A quick look around at the lack of SSS mercenaries seemed to reassure him a little. Charlotte and the others followed him out.

There was an old minibus parked in the field with 'Highland Tours' written on it in large, optimistic writing. The theory, presumably, was that the SSS would be looking for them to arrive in the Cairngorms surreptitiously, rather than effectively waltzing in on a tour bus. Charlotte had to admit that it made sense.

Mediochre Q Seth got out of the minibus, grinned, and made his way towards them. Charlotte did the smallest of double-takes and flicked her gaze from the Mediochre standing beside her to the Mediochre walking towards her. Both were, quite clearly, Mediochre Q Seth. He wasn't someone you could easily mistake for someone else.

"S'up Chaz," grinned the Mediochre that had come from the bus, and Charlotte recognised the voice.

"Rowan?!" she asked, astounded. Rowan beamed and twirled around.

"Brilliant, isn't it? Melz made it up for me. It's like one of her pictures, only painted on top of me, so's wherever I go I look like Mediochre! Not permanent, of course. I made sure of that before I let her do it."

"The perfect decoy," explained Mediochre, the *real* Mediochre. "Someone who looks identical to me, driving my friend's car – who wouldn't assume that that was me doubling back in an attempt to fool them?" he seemed quite proud of himself. Joseph didn't seem quite so convinced.

"Can you actually drive?" he asked Rowan, who looked slightly sheepish.

"Um... I *can*," she said, unconvincingly. "But I don't exactly have my full license yet." Joseph turned to Mediochre and raised an eyebrow. Mediochre looked slightly awkward and shuffled his feet, giving the appearance of a reprimanded child.

"To be fair," he said, "she *is* the best driver I know of who's small enough to pass as me from a distance without making the disguise less convincing." Joseph sighed, fished a set of car keys from his pocket and tossed them to Rowan.

"Just try not to kill anyone," he said. "I'm not insured for that. Not with the car anyway."

Charlotte was not paying too much attention to this however, because at that moment a second person stepped out of the bus. This one looked a couple of years older than her. The sunlight caught his short brown hair as he turned his head to look at them, and his piercing blue eyes seemed to drill right through her and peer into her very soul. The young man saw her looking and smiled. Charlotte felt her breath catch involuntarily.

She was impolitely snapped out of her reverie when Mediochre reached over and clicked his fingers in front of her face.

"It's not easy to get drool out of a school shirt, you know," he said, without looking at her. Charlotte slapped his hand away irritably.

"I wasn't drooling," she hissed, resisting the urge to raise her hand to her mouth and check. "I was admiring him gracefully and in a composed manner." Mediochre raised his eyebrows, still without turning to look at her.

"Is that what they call it nowadays?" he said quietly. Before she could respond, he announced more loudly, "This here is Daniel Boy Snapfax, and he will be our tour-guide for this trip. Daniel knows all about the flora and fauna of the Cairngorms, up to and including dragons, and as an added bonus he knows routes to get there that don't exist on any map." The gorgeous brown-haired guy smiled.

"Call me Danny," he said, in a lilting Irish accent. Charlotte slapped Mediochre's hand as he reached over to snap his fingers again.

Mediochre and Joseph sat in the back of the bus, discussing the next part of the trip and specifically how long it would probably be until one or more of Joseph's firearms required usage. Joseph had £20 riding on it being less than an hour and a half.

Charlotte was sitting in the front seat diagonally across from Danny in the driver's seat, with Dhampinella sat next to her staring coolly out of the window. The Dhampir either hadn't noticed or didn't care that Joseph had hung a sign saying 'Chaperone' on the back of her coat.

Rowan had already set off back towards Edinburgh, with the intention of dropping Joseph's car off at the University, removing her disguise and going home if no-one attacked her, or removing her disguise and stalling them as long as possible before revealing where Mediochre had gone if someone did. Mediochre had assured her that the SSS wouldn't have time to kill her if they captured her. Probably. And I'm good with probability.

Charlotte managed to stop admiring Danny's handsome features long enough to remember the message the tempomancer had left her. Had this been the Danny they'd meant? How was she supposed to find out without arousing the suspicion of the others? She could only hope that she would be able to speak to him privately when they stopped – a concept that appealed on many levels. She wondered exactly what it was Danny knew. And, even more so, how he knew the tempomancer.

As it turned out, they had only gone for fifty minutes before Danny caught sight of a black van with tinted windows coming down the road from the other direction.

"I thought you knew roads that weren't on any maps?" exclaimed Joseph accusingly. Danny shrugged.

"Maybe they use different maps than I do. Maybe they're just lost. How am I supposed to know?"

"I highly doubt they're lost," said Mediochre. "That's about as likely as the SSS dropping the smuggling and going into dentistry."

When the van was slightly closer, a black-clad hand emerged from the passenger window holding something. Exactly what this something was they were too far away to see, but that didn't matter much because the game was given away slightly when a spray of Uzi bullets connected with the windscreen, turning the smooth glass into crazy-paving. Charlotte screamed and Danny cursed, twisting the wheel as another spray of ammunition tore up the road beside the bus.

"Sorry, I forgot to mention the bullet-proof windows," he said, glancing at Charlotte. "You okay?" She nodded mutely, trying to steady her breathing.

In the back of the bus, meanwhile, Joseph had removed the gun in his belt holster and wrenched the handle on the emergency escape beside him.

"I'll accept a cheque, Mediochre!" he yelled as he pushed the emergency escape open and leant out, hair flying madly in the wind, hanging by his left hand from the red handle while his right brought the gun up. There was a series of five deafeningly loud gunshots, and the chatter from the Uzi stopped as it exploded in the would-be assassin's hand. Both of the van's front tyres burst at almost exactly the same instant, and it swerved violently.

There was another gunshot from the firearm in Joseph's hand in the same second as the hand came back out of the window with a second Uzi and fired a burst wildly in his direction. The glass of the emergency exit cracked, and Joseph made a noise somewhere between a grunt and a yell as blood fountained from the hand holding the lever. Mediochre caught hold of the arm as it let go, leaving the opposite shoulder trailing dangerously close to the road as Joseph dropped his gun and Danny swerved to place the body of the bus between Joseph and the van.

Dhampinella arrived at Mediochre's side in an instant and hauled her tutor back into the comparative safety of the vehicle. There was a jarring bump as the bus left the road and stalled. The black van skidded in an arc before scraping to a halt. The doors burst open and out jumped a man and a woman, another man falling onto the dusty road clutching his neck.

Dhampinella leapt from the bus and hurtled towards them at superhuman speed, and the woman raised the Uzi and fired. With a blur, Dhampinella was suddenly a foot to the left and the spray of bullets slammed into the metal of the bus behind her as Danny and Charlotte helped Joseph out and Mediochre checked his wound. The man suddenly came at Dhampinella with a knife, but immediately yelped and clutched his hand as the knife was knocked from it by an arm travelling too fast to see. The half-vampire became a blur of speed around her two opponents, who cried out as a volley of blows rained down upon them with lethal efficiency.

Within seconds they had both collapsed, unconscious.

Dhampinella turned her head towards the back of the van, just as a third man kicked the doors open. From her hiding place behind the van, Charlotte could see that he was holding the same kind of weapon as the security guards at St Merlin's had used. Mediochre had dropped Glint and Desra on the ground beside Joseph and was already out and charging towards the Dhampir, shouting a warning, as a silver-grey stream of tiny objects emerged from the weapon with a high-pitched buzzing. Dhampinella spun on her heel and ran to the left, but the stream turned into a cloud like a swarm of bees and flew after her.

She blurred across the dusty ground back towards the bus, only just keeping ahead of the swarm. Mediochre shouted something at her and leapt towards her. Dhampinella caught him in mid air and used his momentum to spin around, bringing him crashing into the swarm, which exploded in a series of tiny flashes.

Mediochre cried out in pain as Dhampinella screeched to a halt and the man took aim once more with the weapon. Before he could fire, however, something flew past Dhampinella's ear and a knife hilt appeared in the man's shoulder. He gave a sharp bark of surprise, dropping the weapon, and was then blasted backwards into the van as another gunshot sounded.

Charlotte looked up. Both Danny and Joseph were on their feet, Joseph with a second gun in his good hand and Danny with his hand still in a throwing position. They looked at each other and nodded as one marksman to another.

A brief amateur medical examination of all parties involved showed that one of the mercenaries had suffered a fatal bullet-wound to the neck as he'd shot Joseph; the two attacked by Dhampinella were unharmed apart from a series of painful-looking bruises and a couple of probable fractures; and the man who'd been knifed and then shot would probably live provided the ambulance turned up in less time than it took him to bleed to death, but would never use his arm again.

Meanwhile, Charlotte was unharmed apart from a mild case of shock, Dhampinella's biggest injury seemed to have been to her coat which one of the mercenaries had caught with a clumsy knife-slash, and Mediochre had gone from severe burns and numerous puncture wounds to a picture of health in the matter of a minute or two. Joseph had used a Swiss Army Knife to remove the bullet from his hand with the air of one who'd had to do this before, and bound it with strips cut from his black T-shirt. He had another one on underneath, also black, but this time with the slogan 'I'm with Genius' written on it in white, and an arrow which, by coincidence, was pointing in Mediochre's direction.

Joseph's coat was lying on the ground beside him as he worked, and Charlotte couldn't help noticing that there were various marks on it where bullets appeared to have *bounced off*. Danny assured her that this was because it was made with some kind of magically-reinforced Kevlar or something, and that Joseph had had it specially made since he seemed to get shot so often.

"Nice aim by the way," Joseph said, looking up at Danny, who had retrieved and cleaned his knife and was now tucking it into his belt. The young Irishman smiled modestly.

"This is coming from someone who can take a weapon out of a man's hand with a bullet fired from a moving vehicle," he laughed. He looked even better when he was laughing, Charlotte noted. Joseph shrugged.

"Yeah, well," he said. "I was the apprentice of Alexander Gunpowder, what do you expect?" Danny's eyes widened with delight.

"No! Old Mad Lex Gunpowder? Shoot a man for lookin' at him funny?"

"That's the one," said Mediochre, walking over. "He also, if I remember correctly, thought a bullet in the foot was an acceptable greeting in his later years. He died at 72 in mysterious circumstances, with everything above his jaw blown clean off. The forensic experts reckon he was trying to get a scrap of food out of his teeth."

"Way he'd have wanted to go," Joseph assured them.

Danny laughed again at that, and Charlotte felt the need to join in, even though she had no idea who they were talking about.

"Seriously though," Danny said after he'd calmed down, "shouldn't we be leaving? They probably contacted these Triple-S fellas as soon as they saw us." Mediochre smiled like a man who's just worked out he's the most knowledgeable person in a general knowledge quiz.

"Not unless they used a homing-pigeon," he said, holding up his IMP. The message on the screen read 'Blocking all frequencies'. "It's a good thing I decided to activate it earlier and not save batteries." His smile disappeared as he held up his other hand. There was a tiny metal insect in it. "I'm worried about how they got hold of these though," he said. Charlotte looked bewildered.

"Missile bees," whispered Joseph in her ear. "Very clever technomancy. They're like very small missiles that can think, and adjust their course so that they always hit their target. Some high-class security firms are licensed to use them, but apart from that they're strictly military-only. We can only hope that the bee-launcher that man had is the only one in the SSS's arsenal, or else we could be in trouble."

After driving back to Edinburgh without any trouble, Rowan was just driving past her house on the way to the University when she noticed that there was something wrong. Namely the fact that her own front door was gone.

She hesitated for a moment, before getting out of the car and walking towards the house. There were two ominous clicks from behind her. Rowan froze, and turned around very slowly.

Melinda was sitting in a wheelchair a short distance away, hidden from the road by a convenient tree. What was attracting Rowan's attention more than that, however, was the fact that on either side of her great aunt was an armed mercenary, and both were currently aiming their weapons at Melinda's head.

As Rowan gasped and tried to convince herself to remain calm, another mercenary emerged from the doorway of her own home, almost casually grabbed her by the shoulder and turned her around.

"Seth," the man smiled cruelly. Rowan noticed that his teeth were in poor condition yet his breath smelled oddly of peppermint, and that his dark hair had been parted just slightly off-centre.

She realised that her brain was taking in all the details it could that didn't involve the gun, presumably as a way of preventing her from breaking down into insane hysterics. The man pressed the muzzle of the weapon to her chest and hissed, "Where is the egg?"

And then he heard the quiet muttering of his colleagues, and looked down. Rowan groaned. She was near enough to Mediochre's size that the disguise mostly fitted her fairly well, but in one particular area she was definitely larger than him and it was against this area that the mercenary had attempted to press his gun. From the man's point of view, his gun would appear to be pressed against the air a short distance in front of her.

They may not have been very nice, but these men were certainly not stupid. They knew that neither Mediochre nor Melinda could create a force field on a whim, and that there was therefore something odd going on. The man in front of Rowan grabbed her and bundled her against the outside wall of her own house and pressed the gun against her forehead, which certainly seemed to work better. His eyes flicked from side to side with a mix of confusion, nerves and anger. The other two left Melinda in her wheelchair and began to walk towards them, aiming their weapons at Rowan as they did so.

That, however, was stupid. Melinda was blind and deaf, certainly, and so ought not to notice they had left. But Melinda was *not* an ordinary blind, deaf person. She happened to be one of the most skilled iconomancers in the known universe. She had, after all, had over 350 years of practice.

Rowan noticed the faint glow appearing like a thin film over Melinda's eyes, but at the moment her concentration lay mainly with trying not to die. She spoke very quietly to the mercenary in front of her.

"I can explain everything. I'm not really Mediochre. It's a disguise, look." She mentally pulled apart the iconomantic image of Mediochre which was superimposed onto her own body, allowing it to dissolve into nothingness. For an instant her hair was its natural brownish-ginger colour, before it returned to the usual striking red. "If you want the real Mediochre," she continued, "he's gone the other way. I can tell you where if you'd just please *remove the gun.*"

The man withdrew the weapon slightly, and then hesitated for a moment, before pressing it back against her skull, smiling again.

"Nah. They've already sent another squad the other way. I'm sure they'll catch up with him without our help. So really, I don't actually need to keep you alive for anyth-"

He was cut off by an electric wheelchair connecting sharply with the back of his knees, causing him to fall backwards with a cry of alarm. The gun in his hand went off and there was a ricocheting sound from above Rowan, who leapt aside as Melinda hastily reversed.

The loose tiles which they'd been meaning to get fixed for ages now, having taken the bullet as an excuse to come free, all descended onto the unfortunate mercenary at the same time. He dropped his weapon and tried to cover his head with a protective arm. Eventually the onslaught stopped, and he turned to face his new attacker, who calmly tasered him in the chest with the technomantic taser she kept in a hidden compartment under her wheelchair, just in case. He dropped to the ground, joining his two already-unconscious colleagues face-down on the grass.

Melinda surveyed the scene as Rowan was phoning the MIPF. If she knew the SSS, they would already be sending back-up. And that meant that it was now a race between the MIPF and the SSS that decided whether they would be safe. She severed her mental connection to the iconomantic depiction of her surroundings. If the MIPF didn't turn up first, she was going to need all the energy her frail body could manage.

Danny, Charlotte, Mediochre, Joseph and Dhampinella arrived in the Cairngorm National Park without further hassle, of the missile-bee-launching kind or otherwise. They parked the bus and got out. A quick survey of the area established that there were no cunningly-hidden armed villains anywhere within the immediate area. It was beginning to look like they had finally got a few steps ahead of the SSS. Danny announced that he was now going to take the bus back the way they'd come, just in case that distracted the SSS for long enough to buy Mediochre the time he needed. Charlotte, realising that this would be her only chance to speak to him, asked for a private word before he left. Mediochre and Joseph watched them walk back to the bus with almost identical bemused expressions. With more synchronisation than an Olympic synchronised swimming team, they turned their heads to look at each other and raised opposite eyebrows.

"Women!" they said, in perfect unison. Then both looked thoughtful for a second or two, before adding, also in perfect unison, *Human* women!" Both then turned to grin at Dhampinella behind them, who, in a remarkably human gesture, rolled her eyes.

"I take it this is about the message," said Danny softly in his beautiful Irish accent. Charlotte nodded. He leaned forward in a conspiratorial fashion, his intense blue eyes pinning Charlotte to the spot. "Look, it's like this. These Triple-S fellas, they don't just want to sell *a* dragon with TST. They know they'd get much more money for *the* dragon with TST. And to do that, they have to get rid of the other one, if you know what I'm saying."

"So... they've already sent someone up here to kill the dragon we're looking for?" asked Charlotte. Danny nodded, a hint of sadness in his eyes.

"Aye. And not just any old someone. They've got the best dragon-slayer in the business on it. The tempomancer and I, we're part of this... organisation, if you like. They don't want this dragon to die; nobody does, of course. They put him inside the Triple-S to keep an eye on them, and they sent me to you people to keep an eye on you."

"Well... what do you want me to do?" breathed Charlotte. The young Irishman glanced up at where Mediochre was standing a short distance away, before replying.

"You need to lead them to him. The slayer, I mean. Mediochre's a bit of a hard fella to be around, but he knows how to handle people like this slayer. He maybe doesn't quite trust me, and he maybe has his own reasons for that, I don't know, but if you can lead him up that path there" – he subtly indicated a winding track going through a patch of forest – "he'll see for himself. I can't do any more meself, I have things that need to be done elsewhere. I'm relying on you, Charlotte." Charlotte nodded again.

"Of course," she said quietly. "I understand." Danny smiled, and his lips lightly brushed her cheek before he stepped on board the bus. Charlotte walked slowly back towards Mediochre and Joseph as if she was in a dream, the spot where Danny had kissed her glowing warm against her skin. Neither of the men said anything as they turned and began to walk.

· Charlotte tried as subtly as she could to steer the others up the path Danny had indicated before he left. Unfortunately, Mediochre had other ideas.

"This way's neither the quickest nor the most secretive," he insisted, "but it's the one they're least likely to have stationed a lookout on. Trust me, I worked it all out before we got here. That other way, while both quicker and less well-known, has twice the odds of having an armed SSS agent hidden somewhere along it."

In desperation, Charlotte tried to appeal instead to Joseph, taking advantage of his tendency to act first, in contrast to Mediochre who apparently refused even to sneeze without thinking it through first.

"What was that?" she hissed, just loud enough for Joseph beside her to hear, stopping and pretending to peer into the bushes. Joseph stopped and followed her gaze.

"Hear something?" he whispered.

"Or some*one*," she replied, cringing inside at how cheesy that sounded. Joseph glanced at Dhampinella, who shrugged.

"Too much interference," she said. "Plants are living things too. There are definitely some creatures of some description over there, but I can't tell whether they're humans or voles with all these trees around me." Joseph considered this, and then came to a decision.

"Tell Mediochre," he hissed to Dhampinella, and began to move stealthily through the undergrowth, drawing a gun as he did so. Dhampinella obediently stopped Mediochre, who hadn't yet noticed their absence, and explained the situation in hushed tones.

Mediochre looked cross, and appeared to be about to argue when there was the unmistakeable sound of a dog barking, and a stifled yelp. Mediochre remained still for a second, in which you could *almost* see his lips moving silently, and then ran after Joseph. Dhampinella disappeared silently and rapidly in the same direction, and Charlotte, suddenly unsure about her plan, ran after them.

The three caught up with each other eventually, but there was no sign of Joseph. Mediochre kept running; presumably he was working out which direction Joseph was most likely to be in. Charlotte nervously remembered his comment that his ability was at its worst when he was running. Mediochre suddenly stopped, holding up a hand to indicate that they should go no further. Charlotte peered past him.

Through the trees over his shoulder, she could just discern a clearing in the forest, with what looked like a campsite in the middle. There was a gap in the undergrowth to her left, as if someone had charged through it recently. She had little time to comprehend this, however, because Dhampinella and Mediochre set off in a different direction, and a few seconds later the sound of an angry dog barking returned with renewed vigour. They seemed to be getting closer to it.

"Down, Beowulf!" roared a deep, coarse voice ahead of them, accompanied by a sharp whacking sound and a yelp. The voice had a vaguely Eastern-European hint to it. Mediochre stopped dead, so suddenly that Charlotte crashed into him. Dhampinella, annoyingly, managed to stop just before hitting him and sidestep neatly to avoid being caught in the collision.

"No," breathed Mediochre. He stepped forward, slowly, with extreme care, and peered around a large fir tree. "The Triple-S dragon slayer."

Charlotte joined him, as quietly as she could. A short distance away was a large, dark-haired, muscle-bound man, dressed in some sort of bulky fur coat. It was impossible to see his face from this angle, because he was staring intently up into the tree before him, one hand holding a huge, serrated-edged sword. It was probably a trick of the light, but every so often the sword *almost* looked a dull red, like the deep red blood that you always got in horror films. There was a creature which was probably a dog but could just as easily have been a wolf cowering at his feet.

Charlotte heard Mediochre curse, very softly, beside her. Then there was a rustle in the trees behind her, and she spun around.

Joseph dropped lightly to the plant-covered ground and grinned uneasily. The left leg of his jeans was torn, about half way up the shin, and there were numerous scratches from twigs on his face and hands, but he was otherwise fine. Mediochre made a signal and they began to move off through the forest, away from the man they'd seen. Charlotte followed, as silently as she could.

When they'd gone a safe distance and found themselves back on the path, or at least *a* path, Mediochre spoke.

"Come on, stop dawdling, we have to get there as quick as possible." He sounded more like a teacher than ever.

"I thought speed wasn't your main priority?" she asked, confused, as he quickened his pace and she had to jog to keep up.

"That," said Mediochre quietly, "was before there was a deranged sword-bearing monster-slayer in the equation." Charlotte assumed that this was the man in the forest, and presumably also the man Danny had mentioned.

"You talk like you know this one personally," noted Joseph, fingering one of his weapons in its holster. Mediochre nodded darkly, without losing speed.

"I do," he said, and his voice sounded as if he was trying to restrain the emotion he felt. "His name is Maelstrom. No idea whether that's his first name, his last name, or neither, but it's all anyone knows. He's quite possibly the most brutal dragon slayer in the history of... well... pretty much history itself. The kind that likes to stab first, talk afterwards. If at all. He's supposed to be dead. It appears he is not."

"So," said Charlotte, slowly, "why didn't we rush him when we had the chance? He hadn't seen us, and I'm sure with Dhampinella on our side it'd all be over before he could retaliate. Then we wouldn't have to worry." Mediochre shook his head.

"You saw that sword he had? Notice the way it glinted in the light. Almost a reddish tinge? That's Blood Iron. A kind of mantically-imbibed metal. It's quite possibly the most illegal material in the entire world, because a wound from a Blood Iron weapon doesn't heal. Ever. Even when you're me. They're designed to kill dragons, who as it happens are faster healers that even I am."

"Every Mantically Aware Government on the planet outlawed the forging of Blood Iron and ordered every Blood Iron object in their country to be mantically destroyed," explained Joseph. "But unfortunately enough people managed to hide some that it's still a problem in some countries. Unusual to find a whole sword though."

"So what are we going to do?" asked Charlotte. Mediochre turned off the path suddenly.

"Joseph's going to phone the MIPF, and we're all going to get to that dragon before he does, by cutting through the forest here. Most likely he's been ordered by the SSS to hang back for now, and with any luck they won't yet have ordered him to kill it by the time the magic bobbies turn up."

"And if they do?" inquired Joseph. Mediochre turned his head, his face grim.

"Then we hope like heck that we see him coming and your aim isn't compromised," he said. Charlotte would have sworn that the temperature had just dropped a degree.

*

As it turned out for Melinda and Rowan, the SSS and the MIPF arrived at almost the same time. They were waiting anxiously in the sitting room when the back doorbell rang. Rowan breathed a sigh of relief.

If there was one thing mercenaries were not renowned for, it was waiting to be invited in before entering.

It didn't occur to her until she was half way through opening the door that the mercenaries probably knew that as well. And by that time, it was too late.

The door was shoved open from the outside and a blade thrust its way in, narrowly missing Rowan as she stumbled backwards and hit the floor. A heavy boot crashed into her stomach and she felt her lungs expelling their air through her mouth. She was winded, disorientated and she couldn't even see her attacker clearly. She fully expected, this time, to die.

Melinda, having somehow realised that there was something wrong, accelerated towards the door, reconnecting to her iconomantic display of her surroundings as she did so. Her vision returned just in time to see a vicious-looking thug trying to stick a knife into her great niece as she struggled to get up. Melinda did the only thing she could think of. She thrust her hand in the way.

The blade sank into Melinda's wrist and she screamed. The thug let go of it in surprise, at which point Rowan planted a small-but-furious foot as hard as she could into his groin. He gave a grunt of pain and stepped backwards into the second thug who was trying to get through the door behind him, doubling up. Rowan charged into them with a sort of improv-rugby tackle, and the three of them collapsed into a struggling heap.

The temperature in the area suddenly dropped dramatically, causing Rowan and Melinda both to gasp in shock. The second man was a thermomancer. He pulled himself out from under his companion, eyes blazing with fury, and produced an identical small pistol from his belt with each hand.

Then he froze, his expression twitching, before dropping both and clutching his head. The temperature returned to normal.

A black-clad MIPF officer promptly slammed him against the wall, twisting his arms up behind his back. Another one was standing a short distance away, eyes closed, rubbing his temple slowly: the classic pose of a psychomancer trying to get into someone else's mind.

"I'm so sorry, ma'am," said a female officer, touching Melinda lightly on the shoulder. The area was suddenly full of MIPF officers, many of them holding captive SSS thugs. "Those two got away from us." Then she saw the knife.

"Don't worry," said Melinda quickly, noticing her gaze, as the MIPF officer gasped and her hand flew to her mouth. Melinda gripped the knife hilt with one pale, blue-veined hand and pulled. For a second the wound remained; a stark, ugly red welt in the papery skin of her hand. Then the edges knitted themselves gradually back together, until there was nothing there. Melinda slumped in her wheelchair, her fragile body exhausted. Rowan laid a comforting hand on her shoulder, and used her other hand to speak to her great aunt.

They didn't even send particularly adept thugs, she signed bleakly. *And that means that they only considered us a minor distraction.* She didn't need to say what they were a distraction *from*. There was only one person that could be.

"Not to worry." Melinda managed a smile. "I'm sure he'll pull through. He does that."

They were almost at the edge of the forest when Dhampinella stopped, frowning. The others noticed and followed her, Mediochre hesitating anxiously before conceding. She stopped behind a nondescript fir tree and they peered around it.

It was not, as they'd feared, more SSS. Instead, there was a young woman with flowing blonde hair sitting daintily on a tree stump. She looked fairly bored, and kept glancing into the trees. It was also just possible, once Joseph pointed it out, to see a man dressed in camouflage gear lying in the undergrowth beside her with a sniper rifle.

"Dash it," muttered Mediochre. "Unicorn poachers. That's *all* we need."

"Unicorns?" repeated Charlotte, with a touch of disbelief.

"Oh yes," replied Mediochre. "Incredibly endangered animal. Mainly due to poaching for the horns; they're a source of natural mantic energy, used by the unicorns in nature to, well, kill things basically. Not terribly polite creatures, but if you put a young blonde virgin in a unicorn's habitat then sooner or later it comes and puts its head in her lap like a big soft puppy."

"So what do we do?" asked Joseph. Mediochre shrugged.

"Well *we're* going to go give Mama Dragon her egg back and wait until either Maelstrom or the MIPF arrive. Charlotte here is going to save us a unicorn."

"What?" hissed Charlotte, as loudly as she dared. "Why me? How?"

"Simple," said Mediochre. "You keep it away from those two." He nodded his head towards the blonde woman and her rifle-bearing compatriot.

"How?" repeated Charlotte. Mediochre raised his eyebrows.

"You *are* a virgin, aren't you?" he asked. Charlotte blushed slightly.

"Yes."

"And you're blonde. And you're young. Younger than her, in fact, so it'll go to you first. All you have to do is stroke the thing until we get back. Dhampinella can keep you company." Charlotte bristled slightly, but Mediochre wasn't in the mood for arguing and was already walking briskly away, Joseph glancing at them apologetically as he followed.

Charlotte walked over to a handily-positioned rock a short distance away and sat, seething quietly. Dhampinella stood under a nearby tree, without any visible signs of emotion. As per the usual. Charlotte considered chasing after the others, but then again she didn't want to be responsible for the death of an endangered animal, and Mediochre's plan *did* sort of make sense. She just didn't like it.

There was a slight rustling from the direction of the poachers. It was probably just one of them finding a more comfortable position, but even so she peered in that direction, interested despite herself. Until now she hadn't even known unicorns existed; it *would* be pretty cool to actually see one.

There was an odd sound of rushing air and a grunt from Dhampinella. Charlotte turned to look, and saw a dart of some kind sticking out of the Dhampir's chest. She jumped up as Dhampinella pulled the dart out and looked around urgently. The poacher with the rifle emerged from behind a tree, and fired another, identical dart into Dhampinella's neck. She lurched forward, but stumbled before she reached him. Charlotte yelled as loud as she could, hoping vainly that someone would hear, and turned to run.

She got no more than three steps before she crashed into a huge man who had definitely *not been there* a second ago. She stumbled backwards, dodged his clumsy attempt to grab her and fled in the other direction.

The entire area was suddenly full of men and women, dressed in black, holding rifles like the one the poacher had. Dhampinella was lying full length on the ground with about seven darts sticking out of various parts of her. There was a 'Sapphire Storage' helicopter – *an entire damn helicopter* – inexplicably sitting there, another black-clad gunman in the pilot's seat and a small man leaning against the side of the doorway.

This man didn't look very threatening from a physical point of view. There was something mousy about him - probably a combination of his floppy, light-brown hair; his comparatively small height; and his slightly rodent-esque features. Nonetheless, he had a face that could easily be ignored or forgotten, even while you were still looking at it. He was dressed, not in black, but in a cheap grey suit.

What was threatening, though, was his expression. He was smiling in a gleefully nasty way that made Charlotte think of a cat more than a mouse, and not the nice kind of cat that people kept as pets either. He also had an air about him that suggested he was the leader of the others. Possibly even the leader of everyone else, too. He was *also* holding a smaller version of the rifles his men had, but it was pointed at the ground, the arm holding it dangling lazily.

"Don't worry about your friend," the man said. His voice was bizarre – it was impossible to place the accent because it simply wasn't actually there. "The darts only contained a simple sedative. A stronger one than that we usually use, granted, but then she is a stronger woman than those we usually shoot." He stepped out of the helicopter and aimed his rifle casually at Dhampinella's head.

"*This* one, however," he said, conversationally, "contains a mixture of garlic oil and holy water, with, I believe, some salt mixed in for good measure. And a crucifix motif on the dart itself."

Mediochre was on the trail leading to the dragon's cave when his IMP rang. Not wanting to stop now that he was so close, he took it out and answered the call as he was still walking.

"Mediochre Q Seth, this had better be important," he announced. Charlotte's voice came from the other end of the line. She sounded very angry but, Mediochre could somehow tell, she wasn't angry at *him*. Which made a nice change.

"Mediochre. Hello. I've been instructed to tell you that if you aren't back in this forest with the genuine egg in three minutes then the kind gentlemen pointing an assortment of weapons at us will kill us before even Dr Carrion can shoot them all."

There was a muttered string of profanities and the line went dead.

They entered the forest to slow applause. A small brown-haired man was clapping, beaming at them.

"Professor Doctor Laird Sir Mediochre Quirinius Seth, PhD MusD MSc CBE OBE MIMC VC-Bar," he said, "in that order, which I believe is not how they are supposed to go in correct naming." He took a breath. "Well done. You achieved so much in getting this far and then you turned back to save your friends. They could write a story about that. Have you ever considered a biography? Although I think, perhaps, it would have to be in quite a few volumes."

"Where are they?" asked Mediochre, his steely eyes narrowing. Joseph surveyed the area briefly, and spotted at least seven rifles pointing at him from the trees.

"Do not worry about your friends, Dr Seth," replied the small man. "They are unharmed, merely unconscious. I do not like killing unnecessarily, Dr Seth, but occasionally a death-threat is required to make people listen. They are in the helicopter. Won't you join us?"

"You have a helicopter," repeated Mediochre, in a 'yeah-right' voice. The man smiled.

"It was brought here in, for you, under a second. I have... talents in the areas of time-saving."

"You're their tempomancer," translated Joseph, scowling.

"Indeed," replied the small man. "I have been following your work very closely. It is most impressive. But now, I'm afraid, your time in this story is over. I assure you that if you do not come quietly, one of my men is under orders to shoot the girl and inject the Dhampir with a type of Vampire-repellent." Joseph voiced some interesting views on the man's parentage. The man merely smiled.

"Very well," said Mediochre coldly. "We'll come."

"Excellent," replied the tempomancer, and a pair of tranquiliser darts hit both Mediochre and Joseph in the thigh simultaneously.

Mediochre opened his eyes blurrily and raised his head. He made an odd noise between a groan and a growl as his most recent memories returned to him. He looked around.

He appeared to be lying in the middle of some sort of gravelled area. Possibly a car park? No, wait a minute, the ground just dropped away suddenly at the edges of it. He was on top of a flat-roofed building. And what's more, he could recognise the skyline. He was back in Edinburgh. And night was falling. How long had he been unconscious?

He raised himself slowly to his feet, rubbing his head. Also stirring a short distance away were Joseph, Charlotte and Dhampinella. He checked his pockets anxiously. Desra was safe, but Glint the egg was missing.

He turned around suddenly. The tempomancer was standing in the doorway of a 'Sapphire Storage' helicopter. The rest of his goons were nowhere to be seen, but Mediochre recognised the helicopter pilot.

He groaned. Mr Antler, head of the local branch of the SSS, turned to smile at him. The message sent out by his expression was clear: '*I win*'. He was holding Glint in one hand, with the heating charm tied to it. Very carefully, he placed the egg inside his exquisite dinner jacket. He gave the impression he had been waiting to do that in front of Mediochre for some time.

He knew what this was about. They had deliberately let him and the other three go, and waited for them to wake up, so that he would know, without a shadow of a doubt, that he'd lost. And, furthermore, so he'd know that *they* knew he'd lost.

He cursed.

"Shall we go, Mr Antler?" asked the tempomancer politely. Mr Antler flashed Mediochre a final triumphant sneer, and started up the engine.

"Why not?" he smiled, and, as Mediochre charged towards the helicopter, it began to take off. Mediochre ran as fast as he could, but it was as if he was running through thigh-deep water. He could see the helicopter getting away, so much faster than he could run, despite the fact it had been a reasonably short distance to it.

The tempomancer was smiling, waggling the fingers of his left hand. Mediochre knew what he was doing but had no way of stopping it: time was being stretched in this area, so that it passed faster for the helicopter and slower for him. For every second that passed in the outside world, twenty seconds passed for the helicopter and one-twentieth of a second passed for Mediochre. Mediochre could sprint at a couple of metres a second, but thanks to the tempomancer he was effectively running at one-twentieth of that speed. It was hopeless. The helicopter was soon out of sight behind some buildings somewhere on the other side of the city.

Charlotte got to her feet just in time to see the helicopter escape, and Mediochre stop running and stand, motionless, staring at it as it vanished from sight. Joseph quickly walked towards him.

"What do-" Joseph began, and then stopped, and stepped backwards. Charlotte felt it too. Mediochre's muscles, weak as they were, had tightened. His hands had very gently curled themselves into fists. His expression could have been carved in granite and his eyes had become like ice.

The emotion emanating from him was so strong it felt almost like a tangible force. This wasn't anger, which was hot and red and all over the place; this was a cold, hard, focused, ice-blue pulse of wrath. Mediochre spoke, very quietly, the syllables dropping into the silence like iron:

"Get me to a piano."

It had involved a leap into a nearby bush and three bus journeys, but eventually they had got off the roof and back to Mediochre's house. Mediochre was now alone in his sitting room, and the others were waiting for him in the corridor. Joseph was listening intently at the door, and motioned for Charlotte to do likewise.

The sound of the *Tarantella*, played at twice the speed it's meant to be played at, could be made out from inside.

"I've never heard Mediochre think this hard before," Joseph whispered. Then he stopped, thinking. "Actually, I have, but not for a while and that was just the once."

For want of anything better to do, Charlotte walked down a passage she hadn't noticed the last time she was here. It led to some heavy oak doors which, when opened, revealed a huge library, full of dozens, if not hundreds, of bookshelves. Charlotte wandered through them in awe. Mediochre had everything from the works of Shakespeare, Robert Burns, and Agatha Christie – some of which appeared to be first editions – to a huge bookcase containing every issue of DC comics ever published. The complete works of Edgar Rice Burroughs were piled up in a corner, with a post-it note stuck to them saying 'Don't read again'. '*The Very Hungry Caterpillar*' had, for no blatantly obvious reason, been given pride of place on a golden lectern. There was a book, entirely written in what appeared to be Dutch, about the history of the tractor. He even had a case of phrase books for a wide variety of languages from all over the world.

She vaguely remembered Mediochre's comment that he'd analysed Romeo and Juliet to stop him getting bored. She assumed that, having lived for about 400 years, he must have read anything and everything he could to keep himself occupied. It was quite astounding in a way that she couldn't quite describe.

Her eye was caught by a large, brown, leather-bound book whose spine declared it to be simply 'The Dracologist's Guide'. She bent down and pulled the heavy volume out of the shelf. As she did so, she noticed some kind of old-looking scroll behind it. By removing several more of the books on that shelf, she was able to remove the large scroll and unfurl it.

Charlotte's breath caught. It was a moving image, like the ones in Rowan's house. It showed a magnificent red dragon, rearing up, its head brushing the roof of the cave in which it stood, beside a colossal horde of gold and jewels. There was a man dressed in animal skins and leather, wielding a huge serrated sword, standing atop the glittering pile, roaring something at the creature. Charlotte peered closer and gasped. The man was, quite unquestionably, the dragon-slayer Maelstrom whom they had seen in the forest. He didn't have his dog with him, but he was charging towards the dragon, bringing his Blood Iron sword around in an arc.

Without warning, a second man emerged from the shadows, barrelled into Maelstrom and sent them both rolling down the pile of gold, a spurt of white-hot flame from the dragon narrowly missing them as they struggled. This second man was older, and dressed in a larger version of Mediochre's Salamandris-hide dracology gear. Charlotte watched, transfixed, as they fought.

The sword fell from Maelstrom's grasp and clattered away into the darkness, and the brawling men hit the ground, hard. Maelstrom rolled, scrambled to his feet and pulled a knife from his belt as the other man came at him again. They were near enough to the foreground now that Charlotte could clearly make out the man's expression as the knife went in. She flinched as Maelstrom wrenched it upwards, tearing the man's torso open. The man fell, slowly, to the ground, his eyes unseeing, his limbs limp.

Maelstrom furiously wiped blood from his mouth, retrieved his Blood Iron sword and leapt at the dragon as it lowered its head to attack him. The dragon reared up again, thick red blood gushing from a huge gash in its throat. Charlotte gagged.

The crimson waterfall splattered onto the other man as he lay motionless, and soon he was obscured by the stuff. The image started to zoom in, shakily, on the man, as if the iconomancer were running towards him. The writhing dragon tried to scream, and a jet of flame spewed from its mouth, down towards the unmoving man, just as his body filled the entire scroll. The fire must have blasted the iconomancer away, because everything went blurred and shaky for a second and then the scene was being surveyed from further away again. Maelstrom wiped his sword on his fur cloak and disappeared behind the body of the dragon as it collapsed into a pool of its own blood.

And then, after a few seconds in which nothing moved, a blood-red arm shot up, and the man who Charlotte had assumed was dead hauled himself to his feet, wiping blood from his eyes and shaking it from his limbs. He looked around, saw the dead dragon, and fell to his knees in front of it, dejected. He reached out a shaking arm and touched its great head. Charlotte could just make out his tears splashing onto the blood-covered floor.

Then the image faded to black and, when it reappeared, it was back to the beginning. Charlotte jumped as a hand touched her shoulder lightly. It was Joseph.

"That was Mediochre's last few minutes as a normal 50-year-old man, as iconomantically filmed by Melinda Quinn," Joseph said, as Charlotte released the scroll and it rolled up again. "Dragon's blood has incredible regenerative properties, hence why you need Blood Iron to kill them. It entered Mediochre's system through his stab wound, and healed it up.

"That would have been that, except that when the dragon coughed fire at him it did something mantic – fused the dragon's blood with Mediochre's own or something. After that incident, Mediochre had regenerative blood circulating in his own system, but he didn't have the mantic body defences a dragon has, so it started regenerating all the cells in his body – effectively setting his aging into reverse. Melinda got hit by it too, but she only had a few minor wounds on her at the time, so not as much dragon's blood got in."

"That... that was Maelstrom," said Charlotte, her voice trembling. Joseph nodded.

"That's why Mediochre hates him so much. It's not just that he kills dragons; it's that he nearly killed *him* too. But how Maelstrom survived this long, without even aging... that I can't explain."

"I can," announced a quiet voice from the doorway. Joseph and Charlotte looked up guiltily at Mediochre as he walked over slowly and replaced the scroll and the books.

"He saw what happened to me," he explained. "He noticed my miraculous recovery afterwards. After a while he realised what else had happened to me. And he realised what it meant. Immortality, potentially. Something men like Maelstrom are willing to do anything for."

"So... what... every time after that when he killed a dragon..." Joseph began. Mediochre nodded.

"He'd wound himself and pour in some blood. Of course, with him it didn't fuse to his own blood so the effects were temporary. He had to keep injecting it every so often."

"The guy was *mainlining* dragon blood?" exclaimed Joseph, appalled. Mediochre nodded again.

"And there's more, but I'll tell you that later. Right now, I have..." he paused for effect, before continuing, "...a *plan*."

"And you love it when a plan comes together?" suggested Joseph.

The Edinburgh Sapphire Storage Depot resided in Leith, not far from the docks. Officially it was a standard run-of-the-mill storage facility, run by a trans-national storage company. Any inspections or investigations confirmed that this was true.

The one thing the inspections always totally failed to find, no matter how thorough they were, was that it was also the base of operations from which magical contraband was exported and imported into Scotland by the SSS. To uncover that side of it had taken a slightly eccentric but terribly clever dracologist, a seven-year on-and-off investigation and a lot of luck.

Since their discovery, the SSS hadn't had time to permanently move their base of operations elsewhere, and nor did they feel it was worth it. All they had to do was get a single egg back; transport it to a buyer who had already signed the deal; get the money for it; and then the entire organisation could shut down and everyone in it could take an early retirement once their money arrived from its usual laundering. The Sapphire Storage Company could then conveniently go bust and disappear forever. Not even Mediochre could prove anything after that, at least not until he'd been working on it for so long most of them had died happily of old age.

They had, however, taken the precaution of upping their security, now that Mediochre knew they were there. Several patrols of the SSS's finest now constantly guarded the depot, refusing to let anyone in without first showing them a Sapphire Storage Company pass and undergoing a technomantic scan.

It was, however, still functioning as a storage depot, because no-one could be bothered coming up with a suitable excuse to change that. After all, people rarely actually came to use it as such nowadays.

When Mr and Mrs Macintosh, two of the depot's more regular clients, arrived with a huge crate, large enough to hold a person, with suspicious-looking air holes in the top, the guards on duty there knew something had to be up. What really set alarm bells ringing was when three other regulars turned up at other entrances to the depot with identical crates, all claiming they wished to have them put into storage to protect the valuable contents. And when a group of badly-disguised MIPF officers turned up claiming to be government inspectors doing yet another inspection.

Several groups of guards were busy convincing clients to let them see what was inside the crates. Some more were busy trying to deal with the MIPF. The rest of them, given that this was so obviously a distraction, were sent to permanently man every single possible entrance to the plot of land in which the depot stood.

This was why there was no-one left paying attention to notice when a different person unstrapped themselves from the bottom of each client's car as they sat innocently in the car park, and all strode purposefully through the nearest door.

The actual storage rooms used by the SSS for storing contraband were only accessible via a trap door in the floor of one of the empty storage rooms up top, which would only open if the correct code was punched into the keypad that was meant to unlock the room itself, and then a known SSS-member placed their hand on it. This happened quite regularly, and no-one took any notice of it. Certainly no-one stopped to check whether the SSS member in question was doing it of their own accord or because they had been ambushed in a corridor and currently had a gun barrel pressed against their neck.

Mr Antler was being informed of the situation up top by three low-ranking SSS members. There was no-one else in the room when one of the many doors burst open.

Nevertheless, the four people in the room had fast enough reflexes that by the time Mediochre, Joseph, Dhampinella and Charlotte had reached them, each pointing one of Joseph's guns at one of them, they had all each drawn a firearm themselves and now had it pointed at the same person who was pointing one at them.

"We appear to have reached a stalemate, Mr Antler," noted Mediochre, his weapon not wavering from Antler's face. Antler merely smiled, and without warning all five of the other doors into the room burst open and several more armed SSS members ran in, each with their weapon out and pointed at one of Mediochre's group.

"Check," said Antler. Dhampinella yawned, very slowly and deliberately, making sure everyone in the room noticed her elongated canines. Many of them actually took an involuntary step away from her.

"Counter-check," she said lazily. Antler smiled again, and a blur of speed, even faster than Dhampinella could travel, entered the room, stopped behind her and reformed into the tempomancer, holding a knife to her throat.

"Mate in five," the tempomancer said brightly. Mediochre sighed, briefly removed his gun from Antler's face and blew off his own finger. He winced in pain, but immediately afterwards it gradually grew back until there was no sign of damage.

"Mate in three?" he suggested. Antler nodded thoughtfully, and then clicked his fingers. Another SSS member entered, holding Glint the egg in one hand and a gun in the other. He carefully placed Glint on the ground and aimed the gun at it. He clicked off the safety.

"If I get shot I won't be needing this egg." Antler said. "Even if not... that dragon can always lay us another one." He chuckled when he saw the look on Mediochre's face.

"Checkmate?" he asked. Mediochre dropped his weapon.

"Black resigns," he said.

Charlotte, Mediochre, Joseph and Dhampinella sat in four hard wooden chairs in a locked storage room. They had little other choice, because the SSS goons had tied them there with cable-ties at the wrists, elbows, ankles and half way up the shins. These were the same sort of tough plastic bonds used by the military to ensure prisoners didn't escape. Short of dislocating every bone in their limbs, there was no way they were going anywhere anytime soon. Mr Antler liked his enemies to know when they *really had* lost.

As an added precaution, they had been stripped of everything that might be of use to them should they escape: Joseph's guns, Mediochre's various interesting objects he kept in his pockets, their IMPs, even their belts, jackets, the school tie still in Charlotte's pocket and Mediochre's hat. Charlotte was still trying to work out a possible escape situation that somehow involved a hat. Unless Mediochre was secretly Oddjob in disguise, it seemed unlikely.

"So," said Joseph, in a sarcastically conversational voice. "What exactly are the chances of us getting out of here before they decide to free us?" Mediochre, now dressed only in his salamandris-hide trousers and a long-sleeved white shirt, looked pensively at the ceiling.

"Astonishingly similar to the chances of Kitty Pryde being a real person," he said at last.

"Who?" asked Charlotte, bewildered. Joseph rolled his eyes.

"Shadowcat. From X-Men. Once Mediochre'd memorised and analysed all of Shakespeare and Poe he moved onto Marvel Comics."

"Indeed," said Mediochre, wrinkling his nose slightly. "The only real trouble is that I have this terribly annoying itch at the very tip of my nose. And the odds of them releasing me for just long enough to scratch it are *less* than the chances of Marvel Comics being the truth."

"Mediochre?" asked Charlotte. The dracologist turned his head to see her. "That... iconomancy... picture thing. Did... Has... Who else knows?" Mediochre adopted a suitably thoughtful expression.

"Me. Maelstrom. Melz. Joseph. Anyone Maelstrom told. Kiwi Mashuga. Dhampinella, I assume, given she's listening to this. You. A couple of dead people. That's the whole set, I think."

"Oh," said Charlotte. "I'm... sorry." Mediochre smiled sadly at her.

"Don't worry about it." He looked back at the door, and began to hum Beethoven's 4th Symphony softly.

But in his head, Mediochre was counting the seconds, as accurately as he could.

For want of anything else to do, Mr Antler dropped the assorted confiscated possessions of his prisoners into a handy empty box and made a mental note to get someone to incinerate them later.

Had he remained with them for long enough, he would have noticed when a small fieldmouse emerged from the depths of one of the confiscated coats, crawled over to one of the discarded IMPs, and stepped on the keypad.

Some things are easier to teach than others, and the common fieldmouse was right up there with delinquents and trees on the list of living things that take a lot of work to train. Nevertheless, if you persist enough, it is possible to teach one to activate an emergency protocol by stepping on the right key when it hears a certain note, of a frequency that humans can't hear. It is possible to set an Intrusively Mantic 'Phone to make such a noise after a certain time period.

Mr Antler was not a stupid man. Mediochre knew this. A stupid man would not have noticed that running in with weapons was not Mediochre's style, and would have assumed that he had foiled the plan once he stopped this. A man of average intelligence would realise that this was probably a distraction or a trap, and so would have killed him straight off rather than risk a renewed attack from within. A clever man would reach the conclusion that Mediochre was deliberately doing something which was not his style in an attempt to surprise his enemies and, having foiled this plot, would assume they had beaten him and would have no reason not to keep him alive to gloat.

It took a very clever man to factor in the possibility that Mediochre already knew which of the above three you were, and had tailored his plan to fit. Mediochre knew himself to be a very clever man, and as such he had correctly identified Antler as a clever man.

Ever since he'd set the timer on Chips before they'd set off to find the Sapphire Storage Company's four best clients, he had been counting how many seconds had elapsed. The fact that most of the IMP's functions had been switched off upon confiscation didn't matter when he had a pet that could switch them back on. As such, he knew exactly when the IMP sent out a signal that deactivated all security cameras in the area. He laughed, and began twisting his left hand in just the right way.

"What's so funny?" asked Charlotte, raising an eyebrow. Mediochre turned his head again.

"You know what the MIMC at the end of my name means?" he asked. Charlotte shook her head.

There was a very quiet popping sound from his hand, and he slid it gradually out of the cable-tie at his wrist. "It's 'Member of the Inner Magic Circle'," he said. "Member number 302, in fact. Escapology training comes with the title." And with that he shook his hand in such a way that all the bones relocated themselves, wriggled his arm until a flick-knife emerged from his sleeve, slid it out of the elbow cable-tie which had in fact been tightened around the knife as well as his arm, and quickly cut his remaining bonds.

"I thought there were only 300 members of the IMC?" asked Charlotte. Mediochre winked as he moved over to her and placed the knife over the cable-tie at her right wrist.

"So do all 301 of the other members. You wouldn't believe the trouble we have keeping it a secret at Circle parties."

A storage room door is designed to do many things, but resist being opened from the inside is not one of them. Resist being opened by a Dhampir, as it turned out, is also not one of them.

Without her coat on, Dhampinella was wearing a black vest top which allowed for maximum movement of her strong, lean arms if necessary. Her muscles visibly rippled as she forced the door open. Charlotte felt a sudden pang of sympathy for the SSS guys she had beaten up.

By running really fast and taking Mediochre's already-worked-out route, it was possible to almost make it to the exit by the time word got around that a) the cameras weren't working and b) their improvised cell was empty. The guards at the door were so busy listening to the radioed order to be on the lookout that they didn't notice Dhampinella and Joseph approaching them from behind until it was too late.

Joseph looked at the items he'd found in their pockets, including several sets of keys. He looked up at the 'Sapphire Storage' trucks in the company car park, around which were standing various disgruntled Sapphire Storage clients who had been promised quite a lot of money to deliver some crates here and were still waiting around for him to pay them.

He grinned.

Mr Antler burst out of the doors, radio still in hand, determined to discover why the guards hadn't responded. Several SSS members followed him, weapons out, trying to look competent.

When he saw the four trucks missing, he cursed loudly, and bellowed at the nearest underling to check where they were. The underling in question, having had the foresight to bring a palmtop computer with a function that could track the company vehicles by identification chips in them, set to work, and discovered that the trucks were already some distance away, heading in the rough direction of the road that would lead back to the Cairngorms.

Screaming in frustration, Antler ordered the guards to get in the helicopter and follow them, and to radio every spare man they had and set them on the trail as well. He himself charged back through the depot, heading straight for the secret storage room in which the egg had been stashed.

How could they have got to it and escaped undetected in that time? What had Mediochre done now? Why hadn't they just killed him when they'd had the chance?

Once the guards had all gone, Joseph stuck his head out of the bush.

"Gee, look at that, they're leaving," he observed, in mock surprise. "I wonder why." There was an answering grunt from one of the bound-and-gagged guards hidden in the bush with him. "Hey," he said, standing up. "You don't think it could be something to do with the fact I paid those nice people extra to drive away in their trucks, do ya? You don't think they mistook them for us getting away?"

The second grunt was more aggressive, and accompanied by a clumsy attempt to kick him. Joseph smiled, and ran back towards the entrance.

Charlotte ran through the near-deserted corridors once she was sure all the guards had already run past her hiding place. She met Joseph running in from a side corridor half way to the storage room Mediochre had directed her to.

"Fun?" asked Joseph, between breaths, as they ran.

"Certainly... exiting," she replied, smiling.

"That's life as a bringer-to-justice of bad guys for ya," grinned Joseph. "Not for those with high blood pressure or who can't handle adrenaline."

They reached the door of the storage room without meeting anyone, and Joseph swiped a stolen ID card through the lock. It bleeped and requested a number code in an even-tempered voice, at which point Joseph smashed it open and hotwired the locking system.

"Good thing they didn't think to put it in the high-security section, or that wouldn't have worked," noted Joseph as he perused the boxes inside the room. "Here we are," he said, producing his coat from a box. "Correct as usual, Mr Seth." He put the coat on and replaced his many firearms, before stepping back and gesturing graciously at the box.

Then there was a blur, and he was gone. Charlotte yelped, and ran out into the corridor, looking left and right desperately.

Mr Antler shoved through the crowds of people running in the opposite direction and arrived at the desired storage room. He quickly unlocked and opened it, and ran inside, unlocking the correct strongbox on the opposite wall and yanking it open.

The egg and its heating charm were sitting snugly inside. No signs that they had been moved or touched. He lifted them out carefully, and checked. They were both real.

At a sudden sound behind him, he dropped both back into the strongbox and whirled around, producing a knife from somewhere as he did so.

"Ah, thank you," said Mediochre, bringing his hands down on the knife so that the cable-tie binding them together snapped in two.

Joseph was dropped to the floor in an unrecognised room by the burly man who until a second ago had been holding him in a vice-like grip. He shook his head to clear it, and looked around to see the tempomancer sitting calmly at a nearby table.

"What the-? What the hell just happened?" he demanded. The tempomancer smiled.

"You were kidnapped in roughly the time it took a tossed coin to land, is what *happened*, Dr Carrion. But of course, the comparison does not really stand up since all time is relative."

"Lunchtime doubly so?" quoted Joseph, unimpressed. The tempomancer's expression did not change.

"I believe that the actual quote is that time is an *illusion*, Dr Carrion. But I did not bring you here to discuss Douglas Adams."

Having finally had enough of this smug maniac, Joseph drew and fired a pistol from his belt faster than a striking cobra. The bullet slowed down dramatically in mid-air, so that by the time it reached the tempomancer he had ample opportunity to lean aside and allow it to pass.

"I did not bring you here so that I could be shot at either, Dr Carrion," he said, no hint of expression in his voice save a mild amusement. "I brought you here because I wished to make to you a proposal."

"Sorry, mate," shrugged Joseph. "I don't swing that way." The tempomancer did not react.

"An effective if obvious pun, Dr Carrion. But my intentions here are not a laughing matter. I wish to make you an offer, in private, with no-one around to cloud your judgement."

"Won't the gorilla behind me cloud my judgement?" asked Joseph, raising an unenthusiastic eyebrow.

"What gorilla?" asked the tempomancer, without even a flicker of humour crossing his face. Joseph risked a peek over his shoulder. The man had indeed vanished.

"Very well," he said, attempting to retain his dignity. "Tell me more of this proposal, Mr...?" he tailed off, inviting the tempomancer to finish the sentence. He didn't.

"I am here as a... representative of an organisation," explained the tempomancer levelly. "Our intentions are a little hard to describe, so allow me to make an analogy. Consider the Tower of Babel. You are familiar with the story?"

"Ye-es," replied Joseph, uncertainly, trying to work out where this was going. The tempomancer pressed on.

"Excellent. Consider this, then: imagine the Tower had been built. The entire multiple-language curse never initiated. Logically, the Tower's construction would have continued until the

Babelites could continue no more. But think not just of the Tower itself, but of its effects. As they got higher, the Babelites would have discovered so much: the fact that the atmosphere got thinner the higher one went, the curvature of the Earth, a vast number of physical laws needed to keep such a structure upright, and so on. They would have noticed all this, and they would have asked questions. They would have sought answers.

"The entirety of the human race's scientific development happened so much slower in reality than it would have done then. And all for the want of a French Dictionary. I exaggerate, of course, as it would have taken much more than that, but the point still stands. Enchantments exist today which can translate for everyone in an area simultaneously; had they existed then, history would have taken a different course.

"My point here is this: very soon, another Tower of Babel is going, metaphorically, to be built. Another opportunity to advance the human race beyond anything that was once thought believable is arising. The organisation which I represent knows this, and knows also that this time, there must be no interference – nothing must stand in its way. For this reason, we have set up an action plan, which we are already carrying out. We are going to provide the much-needed French Dictionary, Dr Carrion. And it will all be easier with your help."

As the tempomancer brought his monologue to a close, Joseph furrowed his brow, going over the story in his head.

"So... why are you helping the Triple-S?" he asked. The tempomancer steepled his fingers in front of his face.

"Isn't it obvious? That is a necessary part of the plan. Not a nice part, perhaps, but it has to be done. Sometimes sacrifices must be made." There was something about the way he said that last sentence that made up Joseph's mind. The image of an older Mediochre weeping at the head of a murdered dragon swam through his brain.

"Well?" prompted the tempomancer. "Do you have an answer for me?"

"Damn straight I do!" yelled Joseph, spraying a hail of bullets in the tempomancer's direction and kicking the door behind him, hard, just under the handle.

The lock gave and Joseph charged outside, careering straight into the gorilla from earlier. The burly man tried to close his strong arms around Joseph, but was distracted by a swift uppercut to the chin. Joseph simultaneously brought his left knee up sharply and his left arm down hard, one connecting with a groin, the other with a stomach. The big man stepped backwards, almost-but-not-quite folding up. Joseph slapped him hard across the face with his other hand and the big man overbalanced and collapsed.

Joseph ran.

Charlotte ran desperately through the corridors, trying to work out where the others were. She had Desra and Chips in opposite pockets and had put on Mediochre's Salamandris-hide coat. The body-warmer was draped over her shoulder as she ran, and the hat had been folded up and put in her back pocket.

She stopped briefly at a junction, trying to decide which way to turn, and felt a hand touch her shoulder.

She turned around rapidly, swinging her arm at the person behind her, but stopped with her hand inches from his face when she recognised him.

"Danny?" she exclaimed, louder than she'd intended. Then, quieter, "What are you doing here?"

"It's complicated," said Danny in his beautiful Irish accent, gently pushing her arm down. "I had to carry out a favour for the organisation, you know, the one that sent me to you. What are *you* doing here?"

"They stole the egg," said Charlotte. Danny drew in a sharp intake of breath.

"Oh no! I'm so sorry, I should've been there..."

"It's not your fault," Charlotte assured him. "There were too many of them anyway. And..." suddenly she stopped. "They had the tempomancer. I thought he said he was on your side?!" Danny nodded, his piercing blue eyes full of sadness.

"He was. But he's not any more. He tricked us, Charlotte. That's why they sent me here. But first," he said, straightening up, "our priority is now that egg, not him." He flashed Charlotte a dazzling, tender smile. Charlotte couldn't help but smile back.

Mediochre was trying hard to stall Antler for as long as possible. The man had him at knife point, backed up against a corner of the room, but Mediochre didn't intend to be stabbed if he could help it.

"Do you know, by any chance," he said, conversationally, "that your dragon-slayer is almost 400 years old? You do? I thought so. It was a bit of a puzzler when I first saw him, but since I like puzzles so much, it didn't take me too long to find a solution." Antler didn't reply. He didn't even move. Mediochre ploughed ahead.

"You see, here's what I reckon happened. Maelstrom witnessed a certain incident, in which I was healed by a miraculous wound, and furthermore, he noticed that after this incident I stopped aging in the normal direction. So, naturally he puts two and two together, and replicates the effects of the incident on a small scale with his own body, on a regular basis. The guy stops aging.

"But, more importantly, he's found himself an opportunity to disappear. Once a person's been missing for 50 years or so, everyone assumes he's dead, with the possible exception of Elvis Presley. Now, disappearing was a lot easier in those days, before we had the sophisticated ways of collecting census data and so forth that we have now. And with the secret to eternal life on his side, he just had to keep a low profile for long enough that everyone reasons he would have died of old age anyway, and suddenly he's free from being hunted by people like me.

"All he has to do is kill a dragon every so often to replenish his dragon's blood stocks and he can continue indefinitely, and without ever taking part in any form of census or registration, no-one even knows he exists. Whenever they try to register him, he moves across a border. He slips through the system like krill through a salmon net. Ooh, I like that analogy." He stopped to consider for a moment, before continuing.

"Anyway, somehow he ends up in the USA in the present day, or near enough, and there he finds out that he hasn't gone as unnoticed as he'd hoped. Everyone leaves traces, even if they aren't official, and for a company that's used to having to remove all traces of its operations it isn't difficult to notice these traces of other people. The SSS gradually come to realise that the most infamous monster-slayer of all time is right now sitting in an apartment in New York" – he said these last two words in a mock-Bugsy Malone accent – "and it couldn't have come at a better time.

"The SSS were, at this point, running low on business, dangerously near to having to close down. And then, suddenly, they find a brand new market: killing dragons and selling their highly-mantic organs for use in illegal mancy. But to do that, they need to get their hands on a dragon killer."

Antler lunged forwards before he could continue, so Mediochre ducked under the arm and continued babbling as the large blond man backed him into the *other* corner.

"So, they kidnap Maelstrom. But this causes a problem, because while it's easy enough with mancy to make someone vanish without a trace, the mantic governments tend to be on the lookout for such shenanigans. Which leads us on to the age old philosophy: Where's the best place to hide a man? In a big bunch of other men of course.

"By the same token, the best place to hide the *disappearance* of a man, is in a big bunch of disappearances. There was a spate of probably-mantic kidnappings in NY a short while back. It made the news. In such a large number of disappearing people from all walks of life, no-one's going to notice the mysterious vanishing of one man who doesn't officially exist anyway. What *didn't* make the news right away was when the government of Mantically Aware New Zealand discovered a large group of illegal American immigrants with no recollection of what had happened to them. But later, having now discovered that they had all been found, the people working on the kidnapping case didn't notice that our friend Maelstrom was still missing. Remind me to buy Foynitcha Dave a drink for helping work that bit out."

"What does any of this matter?" snarled Antler, still not remembering the knife in his hand.

"I'm getting there, I'm getting there," replied Mediochre. "Let me finish. See, obviously Maelstrom accepts your offer. How could he refuse? He's being paid to do the very thing he does anyway: murder dragons. The only trouble arises when you order him *not* to murder a dragon. Which I know you have done, because that Mama Dragon up there's a lot more valuable to you if she can keep on having more eggs. How much does a TST egg cost nowadays? Certainly enough to let you all live in luxury for the rest of your lives.

"But what if it gets broken, or dies, or is stolen by a troublesome dracologist? The SSS always like to have a back-up plan, so they'd order their pet slayer not to kill Mama, just in case they needed to get their hands on another egg to keep their dream of caviar and champagne and a mansion in the Bahamas alive."

"What's your *point,* man?" roared Antler, the knife coming dangerously close to Mediochre's neck.

"My point," explained Mediochre, "is this: When was the last time you saw Maelstrom?" Antler stared, uncomprehending, for a second, before realising what Mediochre was driving at.

As a terrible realisation dawned on Antler's face, Mediochre brought both arms up in a double-fisted uppercut that sent the knife flying into the air.

"Ow," he said, rubbing his knuckles. Antler punched him.

Danny was backed up against the wall next to a junction, listening to the sounds of speaking from around the corner. When they seemed to fade away, he motioned to Charlotte and they ran silently around and into the adjoining corridor.

Two men stepped out from a doorway, one grabbing Charlotte, the other seizing Danny by the collar of his crisp white shirt. Charlotte was too surprised to break free in time, and her struggling didn't seem to loosen the man's grip. Desperately, she kicked backwards with her heel as hard as she could, and she felt it connect with a shin-bone. The man was distracted for long enough that she could rock her head forward and then jerk it back hard. She heard a muffled grunt of pain as it made contact and felt the grip loosen slightly, and by throwing her full weight forwards she managed to break free.

She stumbled against the wall, and the man swore at her and pulled a gun from a holster on his hip. He clicked off the safety and brought it up so that it pointed at her face.

Before either of them could do anything, however, the man gave a loud cry, arching his back, the gun dropping from his fingers. Danny was standing behind him, a grim look on his face, as the man clutched the wall to prevent himself from falling. Danny's knife was sticking out of his back, and his black uniform was already stained by a widening darker patch. The other man was sprawled on the floor, a nasty-looking bruise already blooming on his temple.

"I'm sorry I had to do that," remarked Danny sadly, as the man finally collapsed, silently, onto the stone floor. His striking blue eyes looked so regretful that Charlotte reached out and squeezed his hand in what she hoped was a comforting manner. He smiled weakly at her, before retrieving his knife and pulling her gently along the corridor.

"Come on," he said, in his old voice, "Standing around isn't finding us that egg, now is it?"

They managed to navigate several more corridors without any further confrontations, but then they heard fast-approaching footsteps coming from a side-corridor. There was someone running in their direction. Danny pulled her kindly but firmly against the wall, one hand slowly curling into a fist, waiting nervously.

Joseph Carrion skidded around the corridor, black coat flapping, one hand still holding a gun. His eyes flicked to Danny with a look of astonishment, then to Charlotte with a look of relief, then back the way he'd come with a look of anxiety, and then finally back to them, accompanied by a manic grin.

"Hey guys, everything going according to plan over this end?"

Mediochre dodged another blow from Antler's massive fist. The first one had broken his nose, the second one winding him before he'd had a chance to recover. He'd managed to avoid the third one by sheer luck, and had run blindly straight into an adjoining wall in the act of ducking past the fourth.

Shaking his head to clear his vision, he stepped back as a well-toned arm narrowly missed his head, and then jumped forward, backhanding Antler across the face. He kicked the larger man as hard as he could in the shin, but Antler merely grabbed him, lifted him bodily into the air by his collar and slammed him, hard, against the wall.

"You fight like a girl!" spat Antler, snarling.

He didn't get any further because something suddenly smacked his head firmly off the wall; very nearly took his head off with a powerful slap as he dropped Mediochre; drove a skilled foot into his kidney; rained a series of blows onto his neck, chest and head; lifted him off his feet by his neck with one hand; and then pinned him to the wall with a single arm pressed against his throat while her other hand drew back into a fist.

"Wrong," said Mediochre, as he stood up, straightened his shirt and brushed himself down. Antler's vision finally cleared, allowing him to see Dhampinella's cold eyes staring back at him, as Mediochre leant against the wall to his left and whispered in his ear. "*She* fights like a girl. *I* fight like a wimp."

Mediochre and Dhampinella were on their way back to the exit, egg in hand, when they met three familiar faces coming the other way.

"Oh, hi," said Joseph, very nearly crashing into Mediochre. "Everything go as planned?"

"Oh, yeah," responded Mediochre casually. "Nobody thought twice about a prisoner with his hands bound following a senior SSS member, and they didn't even *notice* Little Miss Ethereal here." He jerked his head towards Dhampinella, as both his hands were nonchalantly stuffed in his pockets. "Anyone want to tell me why Danny Boy's standing in the middle of a Triple-S depot?"

"We'd love to," grinned Joseph, "but right now we have problems." Mediochre raised an eyebrow.

"The people they sent after the trucks have returned," explained Charlotte. "And the CCTV's back online."

"Ah," said Mediochre.

"At the moment they're mostly involved in a firefight with the MIPF, which Joseph ran into while trying to get away from our tempomancer friend, but they've probably sent someone to catch us by now," added Danny.

"Which way did you come from, Jo?" asked Mediochre. Joseph thought for a minute before pointing.

"Then we'll go the other way and hope there's an alternative exit," Mediochre said, before turning and running.

After running for several minutes, they rounded a corner to be faced with a scene of pandemonium. They were back in the chamber where they had first met Mr Antler, except that now it had become a battlefield. MIPF officers and SSS members grappled with each other in close combat, or sent jets of mantic fire, water, or electricity at each other from a distance, or in many cases just shot blindly at each other. Psychomancers on both sides were crouched in corners, eyes closed, rubbing their temples, being protected by armed guards while they raged their own, unseen battle inside the minds of each other and the other people on the opposite side. Members of both forces ran in and out of the chamber, trying to escape, chasing after escapees, or arriving to help. It was pure chaos.

There was the telltale buzz of a Missile Bee Launcher, and a swarm of metal insects descended on the MIPF, exploding on contact. With an angry shout, a female MIPF hydromancer shot a jet of high-pressure water at the SSS agent with the weapon, and less than a second afterwards another MIPF officer stood up and thrust his hand dramatically at the man. The offending, now-drenched gunman gasped as the water coating his body froze solid; he toppled over like a felled statue and his left arm broke off as if it had been made of glass.

An important-looking MIPF officer with a pencil moustache burst into the room, his eyes flashing, and suddenly all the SSS members in the room shrieked or shrank back in fear. Charlotte suddenly felt an all-consuming, irrational terror seep through her body, turning her blood to ice. She tried to scream, but her breath caught in her throat and she couldn't.

"Phobiamancy," whispered Mediochre, dragging her out of the man's line of sight. Instantly the warmth seemed to return to her blood and she breathed deeply, shaking slightly. Danny put a comforting arm around her shoulders.

"You know," said Joseph, "now that I think about it, it *was* this way I came from originally." Mediochre raised his eyes to heaven.

"I had somewhat gathered that, Joseph. Come on, let's get out of here!"

But as soon as they returned around the corner they had just rounded, they were confronted with the ominous sight of a group of heavily-armed, running SSS members.

Danny and Joseph grabbed Charlotte and Mediochre and dragged them into a helpfully-positioned storage room as a spray of machine-gun bullets devastated the walls and floor of the corridor where they had just been standing. Dhampinella had somehow appeared behind them without apparently even moving. However, while it *had* saved their lives, they were now all trapped in a room with only one exit, which led onto the very corridor down which some angry smugglers were pounding. They all realised it at pretty-much the same time.

"I'll hold them off," volunteered Joseph at once. "You guys try and run past them." He noticeably winced at how terribly B-movie that line sounded. Danny caught Joseph's arm firmly as he went to leave.

"No way, boyo," he said. "They'll be needing your aim later, trust me. And I've still got business here anyway. There's an elevator on the third corridor to the left after you turn right at the end of this one. Hit the top floor and go."

Both Mediochre and Joseph opened their mouths to object, but Danny's blue eyes flashed at them and he made it clear by his expression that he wasn't leaving. Charlotte could feel tears beginning to well in her eyes, but she fought them back.

"Danny, you can't!" she objected, but Danny merely pulled her to him and kissed her, softly, on the mouth. If anything, the second one was even better than the first.

"I love you," he whispered, as they broke apart. There was no more time to talk, because the SSS agents had just arrived at the door. Danny's knife appeared as if by magic in the chest of the first one through the door, and before anyone knew it he had leapt forward, pulled it out and slashed a hand that had been about to fire a gun at him. "Run, you fools!" he yelled. It sounded a lot more upsetting coming from him than it had from Gandalf.

Seemingly reaching a decision, Mediochre charged through the door, ignoring a stray bullet that clipped his shoulder, and Joseph and Dhampinella followed, Joseph dragging Charlotte with him.

Dhampinella barrelled into several of the smugglers in a blur of martial-arts-style fury when they threatened to attack the others, but another horde of SSS erupted from the chamber at them and even she was forced to retreat.

As the fight spilled out into the corridors, Danny was blocked from view behind a seemingly infinite wave of SSS agents and MIPF officers. Charlotte ran, pulled along by Joseph, feeling as if all the emotion and sensation had been drained from her body, not much caring whether or not she was hit by a stray bullet or spell or whatever.

Somehow, they made it to the elevator and Mediochre elbowed the top button as Joseph dragged Charlotte through the doors. Mediochre leaned heavily against the wall, running a hand through his hair, breathing out heavily. For the entire lift journey he remained motionless, his fingers twisted in his unkempt hair, lost in his own thoughts.

Joseph stood still for a moment, before suddenly releasing Charlotte and slamming his fist against the elevator wall angrily. It was obvious he didn't like the idea of leaving someone else to risk their life at the hands of the SSS.

Dhampinella just stood as impassively as ever, her left hand gripping her right upper arm where she had been shot. A droplet of blood, darker than a human's, seeped out from between her arm and her hand and slowly oozed down her skin.

Charlotte felt the tears coming and didn't even try to hold them back this time. Desra crawled out of her pocket and gripped Charlotte's arm with her tiny paws, but Charlotte ignored her. It was hard to tell if she'd even noticed.

When the lift doors opened, they revealed an uninterrupted view of the city beyond. Mediochre stepped outside, and turned around. The lift had deposited them on the roof.

"He did say the top button, didn't he?" inquired Joseph, looking puzzled. Mediochre, however, had just seen exactly what Danny had presumably intended him to.

"Can anyone here fly a helicopter?" he asked.

The mayhem had now moved from the main entrance chamber right the way through to where the high-security storage rooms were, as the various parties involved pursued each other through the depot. In the cramped corridors, long-range combat had become virtually impossible, and the battle had descended into a close-quarters brawl. At the moment it was looking about even – the MIPF were better trained for this sort of thing, but the SSS were fighting on their own turf, *and* there were more of them.

Quite without warning, the brawling multitude seemed suddenly to slow down until they were almost perfectly still. A single droplet of blood travelled, with glacial sluggishness, through the empty air, slowly spinning as it arced between the individual fighters that formed the struggling throng, narrowly missing heads, and hands, and bodies, finally terminating its journey against the cheek of Daniel Boy Snapfax. Who raised a hand at normal speed and wiped it off.

The tempomancer strode through the unmoving mass, no expression visible on his face. He manoeuvred his way deftly between motionless bodies, until he stood directly in front of Danny.

The tempomancer raised a small item resembling a mundane remote control and pressed a button. The storage room door behind the two men slowly rose, revealing various racks of silver trays, each of which had a spontaneous mantic ignition organ, or fire gland, sitting politely on it. A waft of cold, refrigerated air eventually reached the men as they stood, looking at each other grimly.

Then, in one quick movement, Danny reached out and grabbed the tempomancer by the shoulder. And the tempomancer responded by raising the gun, his arm at a right angle to both of them, aimed towards the refrigerated storage unit.

A single bullet left the gun barrel. By the time the gunshot reached the men's ears, the bullet itself had left the tempomancer's small field of normal time and suddenly slowed, but, significantly, it was still moving, gradually, towards the room.

"So."

That was all Danny said.

Mediochre had swiftly worked out how the large SSS helicopter was controlled and soon afterwards it had risen from the roof and begun flying quickly away, all four people easily fitting inside it, when the sound of an explosion roared over the noise of sirens as back-up MIPF cars and medimancer[2] ambulances arrived at the scene of the reported battle. It took Mediochre all of a few seconds to

---

[2]   Medimancy (n): The magic of healing people.

work out what had made the explosion in question, but even that was too late for him to anticipate the second one.

The sheer force of a room full of fire glands all going off at once, triggered by the initial destruction of a single fire gland, blew out every window in the depot and took out a sizeable chunk of the building itself. The helicopter veered wildly out of control as the shockwave hit it, and many of the approaching emergency service vehicles instantly stalled, even as medimancer paramedics and MIPF officers leapt out of them and ran towards the gaping hole in the edge of the depot.

Mediochre managed somehow to wrestle the helicopter into some degree of control before it crashed, and looked back anxiously, visibly torn between going back and getting away. Joseph leaned across and touched his shoulder.

"Let the emergency services do their job," he said. "We've still got to do ours." After a moment's further hesitation, Mediochre turned back to the controls of the helicopter and set it on course for the Cairngorms, as fast as it would go.

"True," he conceded. "We're already running low on time."

"Surely the SSS will be too busy with this mess here to bother ordering anyone to kill the dragon?" pointed out Joseph. Mediochre shook his head.

"They didn't *want* to kill it, Joseph. That dragon's their insurance policy if Glint here dies. Maelstrom, on the other hand... well, he pretty much wants to kill anything that moves. I don't know who sent him up to the Cairngorms, but it wasn't the SSS – they didn't even know he knew the location of the dragon. For once, they actually found this one all on their own."

"So, basically," translated Joseph, "we've got to get there before Maelstrom finds the cave, or else the whole adventure up until this point becomes a complete waste of time and effort, and an incredible genetic trait that only affects a single species dies out."

"Yup," said Mediochre, as the helicopter accelerated.

"Whoopy-doo," came the sarcastic reply.

Down on the ground, the emergency services were working like ants, medimancers scurrying between casualties, picking out the worst and patching them up as best they could before moving on, while MIPF officers escorted the walking wounded to those vehicles that were still working to be eventually taken to hospital.

No matter how hard or fast they worked, there always seemed to be a never-ending stream of patients needing attended to. For those that had turned up expecting only to have to break up a battle and/or deal with the aftermath, it was a nightmare. The only positive point the MIPF could make out of it all was that it gave them an excuse to arrest a sizeable portion of the Scottish branch of the SSS, but of course, that would only be possible after they'd got out of hospital.

Mohammed Ansari, the commander of a MIPF special ops unit called in as back-up when the fighting started, was leaning against what was left of a wall, his IMP pressed to his ear, while his other hand tried to block out the sounds of urgent shouting and pained yelps from his other ear, allowing him to make out the words of MAB MP

James Chrome, officially the most important Mantically Aware man in Edinburgh, who was in the process of having a field day.

"They did *WHAT?*" Chrome screamed, as Ansari related the current situation to him.

"We think they blew up a room of a few dozen fire glands, Sir," Ansari replied, calmly. Beside him, a senior medimancer paramedic placed her hand on the forehead of a man with some particularly nasty burns, and mantically repaired the worst of the damage, regrowing the cells and knitting the flesh back together.

"*All at once?*" bawled Chrome. If the old man wasn't careful, Ansari thought, he was in danger of having a heart attack which, with most of Edinburgh's medimancers over here, would have to go untreated for at least several hours. "How many casualties?" he asked, calming down slightly. Ansari surveyed the scene.

"Um... a lot, Sir," he replied. "But we have the situation under control, just about."

He was distracted by the sight of a nearby medimancer calling urgently for one of his comrades, who ran over and placed his hand on their patient's heart. The original medimancer felt the patient's pulse and nodded, and then the patient's body jumped as a spurt of mantic energy flowed through it. This process was repeated a further twice before the patient suddenly opened their eyes and gasped for breath.

"Sorry, what was that, Sir?" Ansari asked, remembering his conversation with the politician.

"I said where's Mediochre Q Seth?" repeated Chrome. Ansari surveyed the scene. He'd seen Seth's picture enough times to know what the man looked like, and there didn't seem to be anyone around who looked anything like him.

"I don't believe he's here, Sir. Should he be?"

"Oh yes," replied Chrome, a slightly hard edge creeping into his voice. "If a dragon-related crime syndicate's hide-out blows up anywhere in Scotland, all the smart money in Vegas says Doctor Mediochre Quirinius Seth should be there somewhere. I know I told him the case was his, but he could have warned me if something like this was going to happen. This has gone too far, I'm bringing him in."

"There, er, was something, Sir," said Ansari. "There was a Sapphire Storage helicopter flew over us as we arrived. Heading north. As far as we're aware no-one else went in or out unregistered since the explosion, but..." he trailed off. Chrome's voice was silent for a brief few moments.

"North, eh?" he replied eventually. "I'll send someone after him. I want a lot of explanation and he's not getting away until he gives it to me."

Chrome hung up, and Ansari slipped the IMP back into his pocket and went to see if there was anything he could do to help the medimancers.

A muscular arm gripped a piece of what had probably once been masonry and heaved it aside. Slowly, his breath coming in ragged gasps, Mr Antler crawled out of the rubble and into the hot, dust-laden air. His flawless dinner-jacket was gone, and his once-white shirt was now a collection of stained tatters. Blood and sweat trickled down from the base of his chaotic dust-coloured hair, cutting swathes through the accumulated grime on his angry, determined face. There was a nasty-looking gash on his strong chest, and numerous smaller cuts and grazes speckled his limbs and body like flecks of quartz in a piece of granite. A fragment of glass shrapnel protruded noticeably from his left foot, and he dragged that leg behind him as he crawled. The smashed remains of what had once been a communications device hung from his ear, and around his wrist there was a chipped Rolex, the watch face actually split open, revealing the internal mechanisms.

He stopped to rest, peering out at the scene of devastation from behind a perfectly intact door, sticking almost comically out of the remains of the wall it had once been part of. What looked like every Mantically Inclined emergency service member in the city was working their backsides off, quickly progressing through his injured colleagues and enemies. The Mantically Unaware services were just starting to arrive now, and some important-looking Asian man was talking to them, presumably telling them a pre-concocted cover story for the reasons behind the explosion. They'd probably go for a faulty gas main again; that one usually worked.

Breathing heavily, Antler wiped a horrible cocktail of sweat, grime and blood out of his eyes and looked back at the bit of his storehouse that was still standing. It was a good thing they had been planning to retire anyway, because no ordinary company would ever recover from something like this, let alone a company that also had to keep a low profile from the authorities as they did so.

A figure walked towards him out of the leftover building. At first Antler thought it was a medimancer or someone, and wondered whether he should just hand himself over. But then he recognised the nondescript face, the mousy brown hair and, above all, the expression of certain superiority. The tempomancer was coming towards him.

"Mr Antler, Sir," said the tempomancer politely, nodding a greeting. Antler replied in a husky, choking voice.

"What... happened?" he croaked. The tempomancer knelt down, looking at Antler with something that was similar to, but wasn't quite, pity.

"I believe, Sir, that you were knocked unconscious and left in the top-security sector, and that someone subsequently blew up a room full of fire glands in the same sector. We've been lucky though: only six fatalities so far, and two of them were MIPF. It fortunately appears that there were several truckloads of medimantic paramedics on standby nearby." Antler gave a growl, followed immediately by a wince of pain.

"By 'someone' you mean... ugh..."

"Probably Seth, Sir, yes," responded the tempomancer to his unfinished question.

And then Antler's memory of the events preceding his waking up in a pile of rubble came flooding back, and he tried to stand, gritting his teeth in pain as he failed.

"Get us out of here!" he croaked. "Seth's got our egg and that godforsaken slayer's after our dragon! Get me to Sapphire! Now!"

The tempomancer somehow managed to support the larger man as he got to his feet, wincing at every movement. With Antler's arm around the tempomancer's shoulders, they managed to make it to one of the nearby ambulances, moving through the now-unmoving crowd of the wounded and their rescuers, who were oblivious to the mismatched pair who would, to them, now be moving faster than a blur.

It took some time, using the resources they could find in the ambulances, to get Antler back to a state where he could actually walk, and once they had done so the tempomancer wasted no... er... time... in expanding his field of thinned-out time to encompass one of the MIPF still-functional cars, which they quickly commandeered, driving off to see Antler's superior.

Mediochre's confiscated Sapphire Storage helicopter had left the city and was making good progress by the time a similar, matt black helicopter caught up with it. Mediochre could clearly make out the circular Union Flag insignia on the side of it, identifying it as belonging to the MABGov. He had to admit, the impeccably awkward timing of the nation's bureaucracy was fairly impressive.

The pilot of the MABGov helicopter activated a communications link as his craft drew level with the Sapphire Storage one.

"We're within range, Sir," he said. The reply was almost immediate:

"Put me through."

Mediochre's view was suddenly obscured by a technomantically-created holographic image of a man's head and shoulders which abruptly sprouted from the controls of the helicopter. Looking over his shoulder, Charlotte was shocked to recognise the grey haired man in the pin-striped suit who had been at the MABGov meeting she had crashed with Mediochre.

"Jimmy!" exclaimed Mediochre in mock pleasant surprise. "As always I'm delighted to see you but I'm afraid it's not a good time right now."

"You're telling me it's not a good time!" replied James Chrome angrily. "I've got several hospitals full of injured MIPF officers and smugglers, an unexplained explosion in the middle of Leith, countless government officials from both the Knowers and the Ignorants asking hosts of unwanted questions and a famous university professor fleeing the scene in a stolen helicopter! This has gone too far, Dr Seth! Either you return at once and start answering questions or I'm going to have to let the Ignorant authorities go after you! I'm having enough trouble trying to keep them happy as it is!"

"I'm sorry to hear that, Jim," replied Mediochre earnestly. "Unfortunately, if I'm right, which I am, then we don't have much time to capture a dragon slayer who's evaded the authorities for about 350 years and most, if not all, of what's left of the British branch of the SSS, and I'm afraid I'm not going to let this chance slip through my fingers because it happened to make your life easier." Chrome narrowed his eyes, his voice quiet and threatening.

"Very well. But don't expect any help when the Ignorants catch you," he warned. Mediochre shrugged.

"That's *if* the catch me," he said offhandedly. "This helicopter's pretty fast." Chrome snorted.

"Oh *please,* Dr Seth, we have some faster helicopters at our disposal over here if need be," he said, a smile starting to twitch the corners of his mouth.

"I know," responded Mediochre, turning his helicopter so that Chrome could see Joseph Carrion waving at him from the pilot's seat of the MABGov helicopter flying alongside him. "We've got one."

Joseph had slid open the door in the side of the helicopter while Chrome was blustering at Mediochre. The pilot and passenger of the MABGov craft were watching Mediochre and the holo-Chrome's conversation, and didn't even notice. The side door of the black helicopter opposite him had a Perspex window in it, presumably to allow passengers within to see out. He, however, could see another use for it.

He selected the weapon about his person which would make the least noise – a technomantically silenced pistol, which he owned because there were times when even he preferred the stealthier approach – and took careful aim.

The Perspex of the window shattered satisfyingly, causing the pilot and passenger in the helicopter to turn. Joseph took a brief run-up and leapt across the short gap between the two helicopters, hitting the side of the black one heavily and clinging on by hooking his arm through the broken window.

The passenger had left his seat and was staring at Joseph through the window, but couldn't do anything without having to risk causing Joseph to fall which, at this height, would constitute manslaughter. He watched helplessly as Joseph's hand scrabbled around until it found the handle on the inside of the door, and seized it. The door began to slide open, and Joseph swung his weight around until he was inside the craft.

He staggered into the passenger, causing both of them to overbalance and fall to the ground. The passenger recovered and kicked him, fairly hard, winding him.

Dhampinella waited until Joseph had got the door open before wrapping a strong arm around Charlotte.

"Hold on tight, kid," she said in her usual emotionless voice, before she ran at the edge of the helicopter and jumped. She landed safely in the other one, dropping Charlotte and chopping the man inside in the side of the head in one movement.

Joseph got to his feet as Dhampinella knocked out the helicopter passenger, and ran into the pilot's area of the craft. He smiled apologetically at the shocked man as he drove a fist into his jaw. He saw Mediochre turning the other helicopter, so that holo-Chrome could see him, and waved.

"I know," came Mediochre's voice. "We've got one." Joseph smiled as he hit the button on the helicopter controls to stop it transmitting Chrome's call to Mediochre. The hologram dissipated into nothing as Joseph dragged the struggling pilot out of his seat and handed him over to Dhampinella, who held him in a grip like a steel vice.

Mediochre piloted the helicopter as close as he could to the other one, and Dhampinella hopped across with the two men, deposited them in the Sapphire Storage helicopter, and hopped back across to their newly-acquired MABGov chopper with Mediochre. Mediochre quickly turned the helicopter so that it was out of reach for the irate men, and sped away as fast as he could get it to go.

The slower Sapphire Storage craft tried to give chase, but Mediochre knew that the odds of them catching up before he'd done what he had to were next to nothing.

Antler pulled on his recently-obtained new shirt as he walked through the heavy oak doors into the office of the head of the SSS.

"Sapphire," he said, inclining his head in respect. A dark shape behind a wooden desk in the unlit room moved slightly. A pair of hands was clasped gently on the wooden surface of the desktop, illuminated by a small table lamp designed to only cast light downwards, leaving its owner's face in shadow.

"I have heard of the problem, Mr Antler," said a quiet deep voice, a voice that didn't quite ring true as what any person actually sounded like, indicating it was probably heavily disguised in some way. "I'm assuming it was in some way linked to Seth."

Antler knew that the last statement had not been a question. He shivered slightly.

"It was indeed," he replied. "He has the egg. And if what I understand is correct, Maelstrom has gone after the dragon itself."

"I thought I told you to keep that man on a leash, Mr Antler?" said Sapphire, quietly. The voice was not accusing, but the threat was still there. Antler swallowed softly.

"I may have... slipped up on that point," he admitted. "I am most sorry, most frightfully sorry. But, please, give me a chance to redeem myself. Seth will go to stop the dragon-killer, I *know* he will. If I can lead a large enough force there, we can overcome them both and recover the egg."

"Indeed," came the reply. "But you do not have a sufficiently large force at your disposal. All the troops you had to hand are now in prison or hospital."

"Yes," confessed Antler. "That's why I came. I wish to know if there are any of our members who were outside the city at the time who can accompany me."

There was a brief period of silence. Antler fidgeted nervously. Sapphire seemed to be considering his proposal. Eventually, a response came.

"We have some, but not many," answered Sapphire. "How large a force were you thinking?" Antler smiled.

The tempomancer met him as he left the office. Sapphire's personal guard escorted them out.

"Success?" asked the tempomancer. Antler nodded.

"We've got every person we could spare. They'll meet us at a set rendezvous point to the south of the cave and storm it while we sneak in during the commotion. We'll take down the slayer while Seth's distracted, and then we'll nab the egg and get rid of Seth permanently." The tempomancer nodded, his expression giving little away.

At the door, a guard handed them both full uniforms of salamandris-hide. There couldn't be all that many salamandris around with any hide left, given that all their troops were going to have been kitted out as well.

"You'll need these," said the guard as they each took a set. "Now, off you go. Time is of the essence, even with your skills."

Due to the awkward questions that people tended to ask when you dropped any form of aircraft in their National Park without permission, Mediochre opted to land the helicopter outside the park itself and enter on foot again. Mediochre kept glancing at his watch, anxiously, as they walked, and Charlotte deduced that he had probably worked out what time Maelstrom was mostly likely to find the cave.

If he had, he wasn't telling anyone else, and so the other three were constantly on edge as they marched briskly up the quickest track to the cave, no longer caring whether or not it meant they were likely to encounter members of the SSS en route.

"What exactly are we going to do when we get there?" asked Joseph. "I mean, Maelstrom we can probably handle, but what if the Triple-S shows up?" Mediochre looked pensive for a few seconds before answering:

"I reckon we do it the old way."

"What," replied Joseph, "wing it?"

"Yup."

"Fair enough." Mediochre checked his watch again, before suddenly frowning.

"There is no way we are possibly going to get you home in time for you to have any decent amount of sleep before school tomorrow, Charlotte, you know that?" he said. Charlotte was jolted out of her gloomy daydream.

"Huh? What? A time like this and you think of *school*?" she said, disbelievingly. Mediochre shrugged.

"Education is important. I should know, I'm a lecturer. I mean, you think Joseph and I would be doing what we do now if we hadn't gone through a good education system? Three, in my case."

"You went through *three* education systems?" repeated Charlotte, raising an eyebrow.

"Had to. Every 180 years or so everything you learn in the last chunk of education becomes totally obsolete, so I have to get a new chunk before the old chunk runs out. To use the technical terms." He seemed remarkably offhand for someone who was planning to take out a dragon slayer in a short while.

"Seriously?" asked Charlotte. "Wouldn't you rather just, I don't know, pick stuff up as you went along, rather than go through the entire education system again?" Mediochre tilted his head slightly, as though giving the question proper consideration.

"It wasn't that bad. The three separate prom nights was the worst bit; I didn't have a date for any of them."

It was sometimes hard to tell, with Mediochre, whether or not he really was lying.

Maelstrom gritted his teeth as the syringe slid under his skin. It had happened so many times before, and it was at least better than back when he'd had to resort to opening a wound and pouring it in, but nevertheless, every time it still hurt.

When he was done, he pulled the needle from his flesh and watched as the tiny incision healed over in a second. He nodded his approval. It had worked, as it always did.

Flexing his muscles, he checked his newly-sharpened Blood Iron sword one final time, before sheathing it and making for the tent entrance. Quickly, he gathered up everything in the camp, packed it away and left the rucksack leaning against a convenient tree, where he could retrieve it later.

"Beowulf!" he called as he strode towards the cave he had found the previous night. His large hunting hound stood up and obediently followed him, not so much out of loyalty as out of fear.

Together they neared the entrance to the dragon's cave. It was showtime.

Mediochre, Joseph, Charlotte and Dhampinella finally arrived at the cave entrance. Mediochre knelt and examined a patch of ground that looked like any other patch of ground to Charlotte.

"It's been flying," he noted. "Stockpiling meat, I think. Seems to be mainly sheep, for some reason, but there's some deer in there as well, you can see a piece of antler here. It knows it still has young somewhere - it can feel them - so it's making sure it has enough food for itself to last the roosting, and then it's going to go out searching. It's already been searching a couple of times, though, you can tell by the number of markings where it's taken off and landed empty-handed. Since all except one died soon after they were stolen, the telepathic signal wasn't strong enough for her to locate it. Poor thing. She'll be asleep now, saving her strength."

There was something oddly appealing to Charlotte about the way he discerned so much from an apparently normal landscape. Not for the first time, she wondered what it took to become a dracologist. But then Mediochre moved and pointed to some markings even Charlotte could identify: human boot prints.

"It appears that our old friend Maelstrom is already here," he said darkly. "Let's go in."

The interior of the cave was vast, the ceiling too high to see and the back wall indiscernible in the gloom. The darkness made it difficult to even make out each other's faces. Suddenly, the shadow was ripped apart by a bright flare, followed by three more.

Mediochre's face was illuminated by the yellowish glow cast by four of what looked exactly like Glint's heating charm, except that they were yellow instead of red. Had they been less bright, Charlotte would have assumed they were ordinary glow-sticks. Mediochre handed one each to Joseph, Charlotte and Dhampinella.

"We can find him faster if we split up," said Mediochre. "Joseph, Dhampinella, you go that way. Charlotte, follow me."

They set off into the darkness, the bright yellow charms lighting their way. Mediochre was explaining to Charlotte as they went why the cave was so big, in hushed tones so that they would hear any movement.

"The dragon here is actually a fairly small example of the creature – it has to fit through that entranceway, for example, which is only about five or six times the height of a man. But these caves go for some depth under the mountain, so that she'll have enough room to rear her young. Dragon clutches can reach up to twenty roostlings at a time. That's the technical name for a baby dragon, by the way. 'Roostling'. And a group of them is called a 'clutch'. The general collective noun for dragons is actually 'a nobility', which I rather like."

As they rounded a rocky outcrop, Charlotte was dazzled by the light from their magic lantern things bouncing of an incredible mound of gold, silver, jewels and, well, just general sparkly stuff. Mediochre lowered his light and nodded approvingly.

"That, Charlotte," he said, "is what we in the business call a 'horde'. A muckle great pile of pretty things, which the dragon collects. Dragons have this weird fascination with pretty things, a bit like magpies. Hence why Smaug in 'The Hobbit' nicked all those jewels from the dwarves. Not a terribly accurate book, but it got the bit about hording down to a tee." He walked forwards, so as to examine the horde close up. "She's probably got more than one horde in a big cave like this, but this is a fair example of one. Wow, she's got everything here: jewels, coins, bits of armour, an ornate sword, pretty pieces of quartz or other rocks, even some flowers and stuff. I bet somewhere in here she's even got-"

"An actual genuine beautiful virgin princess of the blood royal," laughed Joseph. "I don't believe it! She actually kidnapped and horded a princess! I love it!"

The princess in question was less amused. She looked about twentyish. Her long dark hair looked like it hadn't been washed or brushed in a month, and her faded tee-shirt and jeans were torn and muddy. She had been tied to a stone pillar with some dexterity for a creature as big as a dragon and, while she had clearly been kept fed and watered by the dragon to prevent death and, therefore, loss of one of the pretty things in the horde, she was evidently not in a good mood.

"What are you talking about?" she demanded, glaring at Joseph. Her accent sounded French, which amused Joseph even more: this dragon had hunted down and kidnapped the rightful heir to the throne of a country that no longer had a monarchy. "What am I doing here? What the hell is going on? Stop laughing!" Joseph leant on the stone pillar for support and managed to control his fit of mirth.

"Look," he tried to explain. "Dragons have this bizarre thing about anything they deem to be pure or beautiful or what have you. Usually they just collect stolen gold or shiny rocks and stuff, but for some reason you also sometimes find ones which include pretty virgin princesses under that description. It's in all the myths and legends. Well, most of the more accurate ones. You, I'm afraid, happen to be the rightful heir to the non-existent French throne, and I can only assume you're also a virgin and... well... if you cleaned yourself up a bit you'd make the third qualification. Don't ask me how the dragon *knows* you're a princess, you'd have to take that one up with Mediochre."

"Will you stop babbling, man!" she demanded. "This isn't funny! I've spent the last God knows how long being looked after by a psychotic scaly monster while my friends and family have no idea where I am!" Joseph sniffed and made a small 'hmmph' noise.

"Well then, do you want me to release you or not? I know I don't have the shining armour or the knighthood, but I'm as good as you'll get. Actually, I tell a lie, Mediochre'd be better 'cos he's got half the qualifications." The princess's expression made it clear she thought he was insane, but, as he was her only hope of rescue, she hung her head and tried to act apologetic.

Joseph laughed some more, then produced a Swiss Army Knife from his coat and cut the woman's bonds.

"I'm Joseph, by the way. This is Dhampinella. Don't ask," he said.

"Hélène," replied the woman stiffly, scowling slightly.

"All right then, Hélène," Joseph said, "Let's get you outside. I'm sure Mediochre can search the caves on his own for a bit."

Dhampinella, Joseph and Hélène picked their way through the cave until they eventually arrived back at the entrance.

"All right, *ma copine,* here's where I leave you until I get back from saving your dragon friend. Don't go anywhere; I won't be long, and I have a helicopter parked somewhere that'll get you out of – oh," he stopped in mid-sentence.

A small army of SSS members had suddenly appeared from nowhere on the path, the tempomancer striding along at their head. Next to him, recognisable even through the thin coating of dust, fresh cuts and bruises and dishevelled hair, was Mr Antler. The entire army was wearing full salamandris-hide uniforms, complete with hooded masks that covered their faces, and it was marching towards the cave. All the people were armed.

Joseph swore softly, and heard almost the exact same word hissed in French from beside him. Quickly, he produced his IMP and called Mediochre.

Mediochre stopped climbing over the horde as his IMP rang. He conveyed via elaborate charade that he would catch up with Charlotte in a second, as he answered the call and listened to whoever was on the other end of the line. Charlotte kept walking.

"What?" hissed Mediochre. "Already? That's not good."

"*And* our tempomantic friend is with them," added Joseph from the other end. "Along with Antler." Mediochre groaned.

"Excellent," he said. "Someone with a *personal* vendetta against me. Stay there, I'll come out and have a word."

"I, um, really don't think they're in the mood to talk!" replied Joseph, sounding urgent. Mediochre bit his lip thoughtfully, tapping out the rhythm to *The 1812 Overture* against his leg. Eventually he scowled.

"There's very little I can do," he said. "Looks like we're doing this one your way. Just please don't kill anyone."

"Gotcha," replied Joseph grimly, ending the call.

Joseph eyed the scene. It didn't look too bad; the SSS would have to all climb one rocky slope to reach the cave, and it was sufficiently thin that they couldn't safely ascend more than about four or five abreast. He could, if necessary, take out four or five in the space of a few seconds from this range. The only difficulty arose when you asked whether he *should* take out four or five per few seconds, thus probably making him a bigger killer, per second, than Antler could ever lay claim to.

Well, actually, that wasn't the *only* difficulty. There was also the matter of what happened if they reached the top when he had to pause to switch weapons or reload, or if they managed to shoot him when he stuck his head out of the entranceway to aim. And then there was Hélène. An innocent, untrained civilian always made things difficult.

It was as he was pondering this that another, more immediate difficulty arrived in the form of several kilos of leaping dog.

Beowulf the hunting hound was angry, and scared, and looking for someone to bite. He'd dutifully alerted his master to the location of the girl he'd sniffed out, but had subsequently been kicked for barking excitedly and then sent the other way to keep sniffing for anything dragon-y. Which was a joke. The whole cave smelt dragon-y. Beowulf didn't like the smell of dragon, and certainly didn't like being surrounded by it.

Another thing Beowulf didn't like was humans, especially humans he didn't know were there. And he certainly didn't like it when he became aware of the unexplained presence of the same human he'd chased up a tree not that long ago.

And when Beowulf encountered things he didn't like, he attacked them, on general principles.

Of course, Beowulf's mind was incapable of actually thinking through this situation like this, because he was only a dog. Furthermore, he was a dog that had been mistreated for most of its life by an arrogant and violent owner. Living with Maelstrom is something that would drive most humans to the brink of insanity, and probably had a similar effect on other mammals. The only thing that qualified as what humanity would call a thought passing through Beowulf's brain at this point was:

'*Kill!*'

Joseph reacted instinctively, turning and firing as the shape leapt out of the shadows. The bullet missed the animal and zinged off into the endless murk, never to be seen again. He managed to raise a protective arm as the creature bore down upon him, and its teeth scrabbled and snapped as he crashed to the ground, trying to tear through the protective fabric of his coat.

The dog gave up on that tactic and instead tried to jump onto his face. Joseph's vision was filled with twin rows of what seemed to him to be vast yellow fangs, framing a never-ending tunnel of red and black, populated only by saliva. Desperately, he brought his arm up and across as hard as he could, the gun that was still in his hand smashing into the side of the creature's skull. The dog made an angry sound between a yelp and a snarl as it was knocked off him by the force of the blow.

Joseph rolled so that he could see it as it prepared to spring again, its enraged barking resonating through the gloom of the cavern. Suddenly, the dog fell silent and shrank back. A small whimper escaped its saliva-flecked lips.

Dhampinella stepped out of the shadows, coming closer to the dog. It backed away from her, whining. Dhampinella stepped forwards again. The dog shrank back further. Joseph cautiously got to his feet, dusting himself off, and took a closer (or, technically, a further away) look at the animal.

"Uh-oh," he said ominously. "That's Maelstrom's hunting hound. That means he's probably nearby."

"I can't sense him in the immediate vicinity," noted Dhampinella.

At the sound of her voice, the dog gave a terrified yelp and began to back away faster, towards the entrance to the cave. Before Joseph had realised what was happening, it had tried to place a foot on the rocky slope outside without looking, slipped, and disappeared from view. Joseph ran to the entrance and peered out.

"Quick, this'll buy us some time. Come here, Hélène!"

Mr Antler had almost reached the base of the slope, the tempomancer at his side, a gun on his hip and a small army at his back, when from nowhere a large dog came skittering down the edge of the incline, landed heavily in front of him, scrambled to its feet with a crazed look in its eyes, and leapt.

The front ranks stopped abruptly as Antler crashed backwards into them, flailing at the mad dog trying to attack him. Those behind, who hadn't seen the dog, kept marching, colliding with those in front who had stopped. Before long there was minor pandemonium as everyone crashed into the line in front, several people fell over, the front ranks tripped over those behind them in an attempt to get away, and no-one was entirely sure where the dog had gone until it bit them.

In all this commotion, no-one even noticed the petite French woman edging her way along a small ledge jutting out from the cliff face next to the cave entrance, towards a partially collapsed rock outcrop nearby which she could easily climb down before phoning the MIPF and informing them of current events.

Charlotte walked into an adjacent passage to the one with the horde in it and followed it for a short distance, until she came to a fork. She pondered for a while whether she should just choose a direction at random or wait for Mediochre to arrive. Then the decision was abruptly made for her when a thick, strong arm shot out of the darkness, wrapped its hand around her throat and dragged her into the left passageway.

She tried to shout or cry or do *something* that might attract attention or warn the others, but the powerful fingers crushed the sound from her throat before it could escape. She blinked, and her blurred vision resolved itself, showing her a pair of narrow, possibly insane brown eyes, scrutinizing her from underneath two identical thick black eyebrows. Beneath them, the light from her magic glow-stick illuminated a white sneer of disgust, the shadows cast on it giving the whole face a hideous, demonic quality.

"What do I find here?" her assailant spat, his unidentifiable Eastern accent making the familiar words seem somehow odd; more threatening. He released her and stepped backwards, blocking off the entrance to the passage with his bulk, drawing a large sword from its scabbard on his belt. He was, unmistakably, the dragon-slayer from the clearing and from Mediochre's painting. Maelstrom.

"Seth has got himself a new apprentice, has he?" he scoffed. "A pitiful example at that. Exactly his type." Charlotte tried to work out how far she'd get if she turned and ran. If she was lucky, she estimated it would be about two metres. And if she called for help now, she wouldn't live to call again. It was a *sharp* sword.

Since she would never beat him in a straight confrontation, that only left one feasible option. And that was to talk to him.

"I'm not really his apprentice," she said, shakily. "He just sort of... found me. He hasn't taught me anything yet." Maelstrom spat on the ground in front of her.

"Wants to keep everything he knows for himself, no doubt. Doesn't want to share the limelight. Thinks he can protect all his precious monsters by himself."

"You... really hate dragons, then," noted Charlotte, for want of anything better to say. Maelstrom gave an almost feral snarl, stepping towards her. Charlotte couldn't stop herself shrinking back.

"Let me tell you something, girl," he said, spitting the last word out as if it was some foul poison. "There was a *dragon,* as you call them, in the mountains next to the village where I grew up. It used to take whole flocks of livestock from our hillsides at night, but no-one dared to hunt it down. Then one night, one of the men went hunting and never came back. One of his hounds arrived in the morning, terrified and baying, at his wife's doorstep without him.

"Some of the other men decided then that they had lived in fear for too long, and they set off to put the beast to death once and for all. I was only young then, barely more than a boy, but I went with them, because my father thought it would be a good chance to learn. Unfortunately, I got lost in the forest, separated from the group, and no matter how hard I tried, I couldn't find them again. When night fell, I gave up and walked back downhill towards the village." Charlotte could see him becoming misty-eyed, evidently watching his younger self trudge dejectedly out of the forest. His lip began, unconsciously, to curl up in a silent snarl as he continued.

"I could tell something was wrong as soon as I came near. The sky was lit up in flickering red, but sunset had been over an hour ago. I ran down the slope to the village, the only home I had ever known." He wasn't even paying attention to Charlotte any more, merely staring unseeingly into the darkness, his teeth gritting, his fist tightening on the hilt of his sword.

"The entire village, every single building, was on fire. The cloud of smoke it threw up overshadowed the whole valley. Everywhere I looked, there were charred corpses of sheep, cattle, dogs... people. I couldn't even get to my home; the fire was so thick in that area. But I knew it was hopeless anyway. My family were already dead. The monster had killed the whole village in revenge for our attempted attack. Men, women, children, everyone!" He was shouting now, roaring at Charlotte without even seeing her. Then, suddenly, his voice dropped to a cold whisper, and his eyes suddenly refocused, meeting Charlotte's with a steely glare.

"That dragon was my first," he said. "I ran back up to the mountains, hunted it down, and painted the trees with its vile blood. But I swore then that I would not rest until every one of the murderous vermin had been wiped from the face of the world."

Charlotte held his gaze, too frightened to look away in case he decided to kill her, right then and there. The man's grief was understandable. She would probably have felt the same if it had been her in his position. But if it had been her, she wouldn't have started a vendetta against an entire species. She was sure of that. Grief was one thing; attempted genocide was quite another.

"So..." she said, slowly, praying desperately that whatever she said or did wouldn't provoke him into stabbing her. "You joined the SSS to get help in tracking them down? And now you're going to kill this one?" Maelstrom didn't even nod. He merely spat again. Charlotte swallowed, very gently. She could see from the man's eyes that he was crazed. His reminiscence had clearly driven him even further into madness than he had been already. It became obvious that he was going to kill her, sooner or later, even if she kept him talking. There was one more thing she could try, even if she hated the thought of it.

"Please," she begged, attempting to flutter her eyelashes in a pitiful way. "Let me go. I won't tell anyone. I'll just leave. Please." Maelstrom recoiled, a look of pure, undisguised revulsion on his face, as if she had just presented him with a pile of steaming offal.

"You pathetic female wretch!" he roared, swinging his Blood Iron sword in a circle above his head, and then bringing it around in an arc, the trajectory of which involved her own midriff.

Before Charlotte could do anything, there was a flash of silver and Maelstrom roared with pain and fury, the sword dropping from his hands. He caught it before it hit the ground and swung it at Charlotte, but the distraction had given her time to jump backwards. She tripped over a rock as the blade flashed centimetres from her face, and fell rather ungracefully backwards, rolling to the side as she landed in case of a second blow.

"I may be with you on the description," said a blissfully familiar voice, "but the whole swingy-sword follow-through bit just doesn't do it for me."

Mediochre stepped into view as Charlotte stood up, one hand on his hip, looking quizzically at Maelstrom. Charlotte could see an ornate, silver-hilted short sword, the one Mediochre had pointed out in the horde, no less, biting into Maelstrom's right wrist, so deep that it hung there unsupported. Thick red blood was dripping down it. It was a sickening sight.

Mediochre reached forwards and grabbed the hilt of the short sword, just briefly, releasing it immediately. Maelstrom howled and his other hand spasmed, dropping his own sword, which was then deftly flicked into the gloom by Mediochre's swinging leg.

Quick as a flash, although not quite as bright, Maelstrom grabbed the short sword by its ornate hilt and yanked it out of his arm. The gash where it had been began to knit itself back together as he hurled the sword, point-first, at Mediochre's head.

Mediochre wasn't quite quick enough to dodge the blade. He tried to twist out of its path, but not in time. Charlotte covered her ears to block out his agonised cry as the razor-sharp point sank into the side of Mediochre's head like it was a mere puddle of water. Blindly, he scrabbled at his cheek, trying to grasp the thing and pull it out. Maelstrom wrapped his powerful hands around Mediochre's neck and slammed him into the cave wall just as Mediochre managed to dislodge the blade and cast it aside.

Maelstrom leered into Mediochre's face as he squeezed. His own massive form dwarfed his opponent's small stature, giving the pair an unreal quality. Mediochre's head was already turning red, so much so that you couldn't easily make out the blood on its left side. Charlotte knew how that felt; it was the same position she'd been in herself not long ago. She also knew that, somehow, she had to save him.

She cast around frantically for something, anything; she didn't even know what. Her gaze fell upon the Blood Iron sword, hiding in a shadowed corner of the rock. Swallowing slightly, she picked it up. It was heavier than she'd anticipated; too heavy for her to wield, but she dragged it towards the struggling pair anyway. Grunting with the effort, she swung her entire body, using all her strength to bring the sword hurtling around, cutting Maelstrom's arm as it passed.

She hadn't cut him deep, knowing that the wound wouldn't heal and not wanting to put a man's arm permanently out of action, but it was enough that Maelstrom's grip lessened as he gave an animalistic yell of anger. Mediochre took advantage of the man's brief distraction, bringing his leg up sharply. His miniature knee caught the slayer by surprise, and he was able to break free from the larger man's death-grip before he collected himself again.

Enraged, Maelstrom snatched his sword from Charlotte's hands, and she threw up her arms in a vain attempt to protect her face from the inevitable blow.

The blow never came. Partially blinded by the murk and his own anger, Maelstrom had grabbed the sword by its blade, thinking it was the hilt. The weapon clattered to the ground as he clutched at his bleeding hand, howling echoing curses into the endless underground depths. Mediochre grabbed Charlotte's hand and tugged urgently. Getting his drift immediately, she began to run.

The pandemonium which the SSS army had disintegrated into fell silent, as one man, at the deafening report of a firearm being fired at close range. Mr Antler stood in the middle of the rabble, his gun in his outstretched arm, the barrel smoking slightly. An unmoving pile of fur lay in front of him, unaware now of the gun still pointed at it.

Antler lowered the weapon slowly and looked up at his troops. It was clear from his expression exactly what he thought of them at that moment. Without a word, the troops quickly and silently moved back into formation. Without his expression softening, Antler gave a signal and they resumed marching towards the cave entrance.

A short distance above and ahead of them, Joseph was torn between doing something to stop them and running back to investigate the distant sound of cursing he had heard from the bowels of the cave behind him. After a moment or two, he reached his decision.

"Dhampinella," he announced, with an apologetic smile. "I'm leaving this one to you for now."

Dhampinella nodded her acknowledgement, and turned back to the entrance. Quite slowly, as if it were a practiced ceremony, she reached up and undid the buttons of her coat, one by one, from the neck down to the hem. She removed her left arm, then her right. The coat was dropped onto the ground at arm's length from her body. She shook her arms, and flexed her fingers. Then, her expression as enigmatic as ever, she stepped into the entranceway, just as the first row of SSS soldiers began running up towards it.

The darkness of the cave enveloped Joseph's receding form behind her as the first of the men noticed her and raised a weapon. Then the man was stumbling backwards, the weapon slightly bent and dropping to the ground beside him. The only movement that could be seen from Dhampinella was a slight twitching. The rest of the troops in the man's line saw the Dhampir and charged at her, raising their own weapons. Each one appeared to be hit by an invisible car, flying backwards and tumbling down the rock slope, before they reached her. This time, an onlooker might have perceived Dhampinella's form flicker slightly.

The Dhampir was breathing heavier than normal, but had little time to catch her breath. There was still the line behind to deal with. And the line behind that.

Mediochre tugged Charlotte's sleeve, pulling her down one of the many large winding passages that led off from the chamber in which the horde resided.

"This way," he hissed between pants.

"Why?" responded Charlotte, who was already starting to overtake him due to the greater length of her stride.

"He's less likely to think we've gone this way," Mediochre gasped.

"How sure are you?" Charlotte asked, glancing over her shoulder for any sign of pursuit. Mediochre thought for a moment before answering.

"Forty-one percent. Ish," he replied. Charlotte didn't much like those odds.

"Could you become *more* sure?" she requested, looking at him.

"Have you got a piano on you?" he asked.

"And if I were to tell you I left it in my other jacket?" she said, giving him a patronising look.

"Then no. Forty-oneish will have to do."

Eventually, neither of them could run any further, and Mediochre half-collapsed against the rough stone wall.

"I don't actually think you're a pathetic wretch at all," he said, managing a smile. "Given the circumstances, I'd say you're pretty impressive." Charlotte smiled a little, without knowing entirely why.

"You could have done worse yourself," she said, feigning a shrug. Mediochre gave a short laugh.

It was hard to tell whether he was imagining it, but Mr Antler was fairly sure he could see a faint blurry haze in the air when the Dhampir moved now. Almost as if she was now going very nearly slow enough to actually see. It could be that she was tiring.

"Shall we take her out?" he asked the tempomancer beside him, as another row of soldiers failed to move quite fast enough to avoid being thrown, unconscious, down the slope. The smaller man shook his head.

"If it were me, sir, I'd just sneak past her. As long as she's busy out here, she won't be in there protecting Seth. *And* they'll assume that no-one's managed to enter as long as she's still guarding the door." Mr Antler nodded.

"That sounds like a good plan to me," he said. He motioned to one of the SSS soldiers bringing up the rear. This one was dressed the same as all of the others, but held the SSS's third missile bee launcher. "You there. Come with us. We're going dracologist-hunting."

The man obediently stepped forward and linked his arm through the tempomancer's left elbow. Mr Antler linked his through the right one. The tempomancer twitched an eyebrow, and time stopped.

Joseph saw a faint light up ahead and hurried on. As he got nearer, he could make out the shapes of Mediochre and Charlotte in the centre of the glow made by their lighting charms.

Mediochre noticed his approach and waved. They waited for him to catch up with them, and then Mediochre spoke.

"Triple-S?" he inquired. Joseph jerked his thumb back the way they'd come.

"Dhampinella seems to have them under control," he replied. "What happened here? I heard noises."

"Maelstrom," said Mediochre simply. "We seem to have escaped. But we really need to get to that dragon now, before he finds it." He stopped, frowning. "Hang on; did you leave Dhampinella alone out there with the entire army? They've got a tempomancer. He'd probably come after us before he went for her, but I can't be sure of that without a piano." Joseph shrugged.

"She's a Dhampir. It doesn't matter how slow he makes her, she's still better at killing than she is at dying." Mediochre nodded thoughtfully. After a short period of walking, they came out in a huge dark empty space.

"Grip the light harder," Mediochre whispered to Charlotte. She obeyed, and the other two did the same. Immediately, the glow emanating from each of the three charms increased in luminescence.

They had entered a vast stone cavern, easily large enough to fit a cathedral inside. There were four huge, dragon-sized passages leading off of it in different directions.

"We're way down underneath the mountain now," muttered Mediochre, apparently to himself. "And I'll bet the nest is off down one of these routes."

He slowly walked up to each passageway in turn; bending to look at the ground, examining the walls, licking his finger and holding it in the air, and performing various other unfathomable measurements. Then:

"It's a toss-up between these two," he said, pointing at the two passages at the far end of the cavern with opposite index fingers, so that his arms crossed in front of his chest. "And we probably haven't the time to search both."

"Well, OK," interjected Charlotte. "One of us go one way, the other two go the other." Mediochre nodded.

"It always seemed to work for the guys in *Scooby Doo*," he said. "I'll take the left one. You two go down the right. I'll be fine on my own."

Joseph recognised Don't-bother-trying-to-argue-we-haven't-got-time Expression No. 3 on Mediochre's face, so he merely nodded and set off, his gun raised in case of unexpected villains, just like old times. Charlotte shrugged and followed. She didn't bother to point out that in *Scooby Doo*, somebody always ended up being chased by some form of hideous creature shortly after the gang split up.

Maelstrom fumed as he hurried through the endless caverns, his bloody hand clamped over the wound his own sword had made on his arm. He was now more determined than ever to get to that dragon and paint its blood across the cave walls before Seth got there. This wasn't just about his vendetta against dragonkind any more; it was also about showing that idiot monster-lover and his girl that they couldn't wound a dragon-slayer and expect to get away with it. And, hopefully, it was also about finishing what he'd started 350 years ago: wiping Mediochre Quirinius Seth out of the world of the living, before he did any more damage to the human species with his constant protection of these beasts.

His only problem was how he was going to track anything down when his good-for-nothing hunting hound hadn't bothered to come back.

That and the bleeding wound.

And the fact Seth had a head start.

Nearly four hundred years of hunting had honed Maelstrom's senses far beyond that of an ordinary man, and he could tell he wasn't imagining it when he had the sudden, inexplicable feeling someone had just walked past him. But nevertheless, he had seen nothing.

Maelstrom stopped walking and stood, perfectly still, his expression giving nothing away. He could easily have been a statue, or even just a person-shaped phenomenon of rock erosion.

In a blur of speed, he whipped around and pinned the tempomancer to a convenient pillar of stone, his sword going from sheathed to pressed-very-lightly-against-his-opponent's-chest in less time than it took to draw breath.

"What the hell are you doing here?" he hissed menacingly. The tempomancer smiled a smile so enigmatic, it made the Mona Lisa look about as subtle as a hammer.

"Isn't it evident?" he said, clearly enunciating each word even with a Blood Iron blade spanning the entire length of his torso. "I slipped away from the others to come and speak to you. Oh, and yes," he added, seeing Maelstrom's expression change. "There are *lots* of others. All currently either otherwise engaged, or frozen. At least, as near to frozen as is practically viable. But that will change. You had better get to the dragon soon if you want to get there at all." The tempomancer did not show any emotion, even when Maelstrom growled and pressed the sword harder, so that it cut through the outer layers of his clothing.

"Where is it?" he snarled. The tempomancer sighed jadedly.

"That," he said, looking at his captor with condescending eyes, "is exactly where I'm here to direct you to."

Joseph turned sharply around a corner, sweeping the passage ahead with the aim of his gun before releasing it with one of his hands in order to motion to Charlotte to join him. It must have been at least the tenth time this had happened, and Charlotte for one was beginning to tire of it.

"Let me guess," she sighed as she approached him. "Still no sign of dragon or bad guys." Joseph nodded, apparently not noticing the tone of Charlotte's voice. Then, suddenly, he froze, staring straight ahead.

"Damn," he hissed.

"What?" asked Charlotte, confused and more than a little irritated. Joseph turned to her, his mouth hanging open in shocked realisation.

"If we do find the dragon, we can't do much. The egg's down that other passage with Medi."

"So?" Charlotte shrugged. "We couldn't both take it."

"No," agreed Joseph. "But don't you see? Mediochre *could* tell which passage was probably the right one. Mediochre always *can*. But he didn't want you to go with him because at the end of that passage would be an angry mother dragon and/or an even angrier Maelstrom. There may be many things Mediochre is willing to do for dragons, but putting a teenager in danger isn't one of them."

"He didn't seem so worried about my welfare before, when I had crazy smugglers after me," Charlotte pointed out. "Besides, why did he leave you too?"

"He left me with you because if by chance he *was* wrong, he'd feel better knowing he'd left you with an expert gunman and an arsenal of weapons," Joseph said bluntly. "As for before, with the Triple-S, exactly how hard, would you say, did we have to push him before he let you tag along?" Charlotte considered this.

"Reasonably, I suppose. He *did* refuse to let me get involved the first three or four times..." she tailed off.

"Mediochre's just gone off to face a dragon, a killer, and who-knows-what else on his own," said Joseph, voicing Charlotte's own thoughts. "To protect you."

"Oh great," uttered Charlotte. "Well what are we waiting for? Let's go bail the idiot out."

The shadows in a slight alcove in the rock moved unexplainably as she turned around. Mr Antler stepped out into the light of her charm, preceded by the barrel of a terribly efficient-looking firearm.

"You mentioned an idiot in need of bailing?" he inquired, a vengeful smile playing at the corners of his lips.

Mediochre Quirinius Seth walked slowly out of the passage and into a cavern, remaining in plain sight of the entire vast space, Glint the egg held out in front of him with both hands and his head down as if in reverence.

He reached the middle of the cold stone floor of the cavern and knelt carefully, placing the egg in front of him and gently removing the heating charm tied to it. Still with great care, he removed the lighting charm sticking out of his pocket and placed it to one side along with the heating charm. He removed his hat and placed it over the two sticks, blocking out the light.

His face was lit instead, when he looked up, by a soft, deep blue glow that swirled and fluctuated oddly, almost like sunlight glinting off oily water. A few lone beads of sweat began to form at his hairline and progress at glacial speed towards the earth that pulled them downwards. A glinting salamandris scampered across his hand when he placed it on the ground to steady himself, throwing a scale-like pattern of reflected light across his arm.

Piled in front of the tiny dracologist was an immense hill of glittering crystals – almost an entire seam of quartz, removed from its underground refuge fragment by fragment. The blue light shimmered across its surface. And on top of the horde lay the source of the light.

The sheer scale of the dragon was difficult to comprehend; so much greater was it than the expected size for any creature capable of flying. The deep scales that covered all that could be seen of the creature's body were mottled with what seemed like every shade of blue that the natural world could achieve. A magnificent pair of scaleless wings, their membrane so dark a blue that it could easily have been mistaken for black, were folded so that they covered much of the dragon's back, while the scales became paler in colour towards its feet, where the light blue of the toes merged seamlessly into the off-white of the claws, which could have opened up a prize bull like a baked potato.

Even curled as it was on top of its shining trove, its tail tucked behind its head like an ouroboros, the creature exuded an aura of nobility greater than any rainforest-dwelling savage in days gone by. A single huge eye, like a glittering salmon in the blue sea, focussed its jet-black pupil on Mediochre. It seemed to be peeling back his never-aging flesh and exposing his very soul.

Which, Mediochre conceded, it probably was.

You have brought one of my children. It was a statement, not a question, and Mediochre did not insult the dragon by answering. He couldn't help flinching slightly as the voice seemed to blossom outwards from inside his own mind; it sounded exactly like what he remembered of his grandmother. *Where are the others?*

"I... was too late to save them," said Mediochre out loud. He knew that the dragon could have extracted this information by the power of her telepathy had she wanted, but evidently she wished to hear it from him. "By the time I got to them they were already dead."

The dragon's eye closed for a second. Then, in a single fluid movement, she unwrapped herself from her horde, stood rampant on her hind legs, and gave a deafening roar of grief and pain, tipping back her head and spewing white flame into the air above her, where it pooled against the ceiling of the cavern. Her dark wings spread out until they almost filled the cavern from end to end, and her thrashing tail sent chunks of quartz flying in all directions.

Mediochre fell to the side, steadying himself again with his left hand, overcome by the heat and the brief burst of misery which flashed through his mind as the dragon lost control of her telepathic abilities.

Eventually, she settled back onto the remains of her horde, allowing her fire to disperse, and reached out towards Mediochre with a clawed foot. The sharp, smooth claws delicately picked up the shining egg like a human might cradle a fragile flower, and positioned it carefully next to the scales of her side. The tent-like wings closed over it, ensuring the maximum amount of her body heat was transferred to the developing dragon within.

"I'm sorry," said Mediochre as he resumed his upright kneeling position. The dragon looked him over silently before replying.

I am also sorry, she said. *The clutch's father was killed by humans. When humans also stole the clutch, I was so very enraged. They put something in me, some poison that made me sleep, and when I awoke my mind could not sense them. I searched for several days, but I was still weak after remaining roostbound to tend to the clutch, and before a long time had passed I had to return and rest. But you have done what I could not do myself, and what I feared would never be done. You have saved one of my children. Thank you.*

"You're welcome," replied Mediochre. He had to stop to remove his body-warmer and jacket as the heat given off by the dragon finally became too much for him. The dragon's pupils slowly shrank in size; the dracological equivalent of breaking into a smile.

What is your name, small human? she asked.

"Mediochre," said Mediochre. "There are a lot of other words in there, but that's the important bit."

I was once known as Deep Ocean to other dragons, the dragon replied. *It's a shade of blue.* Mediochre smiled.

Would you like it if I were to name the child Mediochre? It is a boy, as I expect you know. Mediochre was startled, as he always was when faced with unexpected unexpectedness.

"No, thank you, please don't," he gabbled. He laughed uneasily as the dragon gave an amused snort. "It wouldn't suit him," he said. "He's not red."

Mediochre felt the dragon's amusement as she gently eased into his mind again.

You're right, she said. *Beside which, I like the name... 'Glint'.*

"Really?" gasped Mediochre. Deep Ocean smiled again. She knew it wasn't a question, and she wasn't going to insult Mediochre by answering.

Kurt Blackthorn understood his instructions perfectly. If he found anyone that wasn't SSS, he missile-beed them. If he found Seth himself, he pointed the launcher at him and kept firing until it was empty, before sticking his knife in the troublemaker's brain. There was a limit to what it's physically *possible* to heal from.

So when he arrived at the entrance to the cavern and saw Mediochre clearly framed by the blue glow from behind him, he wasted no time. Keeping in the shadows, he pointed the launcher at him and kept firing until it was empty.

Dhampinella was definitely tiring now. A casual observer who just happened to be strolling through a remote part of the Cairngorms in his casual, observing way would have clearly been able to see her running, dodging and striking. She would still have been moving pretty fast for a human, but for a Dhampir she was clearly half an hour at most away from collapse.

To make it worse, some of the first people she'd hit were now getting up again. It seemed to her that every new opponent made it slightly closer to getting past her. She didn't have Mediochre's skill with numbers, but she could tell that she was going to run out of closeness-to-getting-past-her before she ran out of opponents.

Maelstrom and the tempomancer strode past the motionless SSS agent and into the cavern. Mediochre was kneeling in the middle of the wide space, staring up at a huge dark blue dragon, which was in turn gazing at him down its scaly muzzle. A line of tiny metal insects, suspended in mid-air, ran from the barrel of the agent's weapon to a point a few feet short of Mediochre's head. Maelstrom grinned nastily.

"Looks like your boy had the same idea as me," he noted. Adjusting his grip on the Blood Iron sword, he began to walk towards the dragon, before suddenly stopping. He wheeled around and pointed his finger at the tempomancer, who said nothing. "Why did you want to help me? You people tried to hide that beast from me! Why have you suddenly changed your mind?"

The tempomancer sighed and leant against the wall, closing his eyes for a second.

"My motives are terribly complex," he replied jadedly, "and getting you to understand them would be an arduous and time-consuming process. I may control time, but I nevertheless have no wish to waste it. Let us merely say that I am not truly a representative of the Sapphire Smuggling Syndicate, and the institution which I do represent has its own benefits to gain from you killing that dragon right here, right now. Now are you going to do it or not?"

"No!" snarled Maelstrom. "Not for you! I am not a pawn!" The tempomancer began inspecting his fingernails casually.

"Of course not," he agreed. "I'd have given you the position of rook myself. But it makes no difference to me whether you kill it for us, for yourself, or for the entire population of the Former Yugoslav Republic of Macedonia. You want it to die. I want it to die. The organisation which I represent wants it to die. What's the problem?" Maelstrom grunted.

"And what of Seth?" he asked. The tempomancer began to scrape idly at the nail of his middle finger using the thumbnail of the same hand.

"Seth, I'm afraid, cannot be killed by you. Rest assured that he *will* die, but not by your hand. Not now. I'm afraid I cannot allow that. If you attempt it, I will be forced to stop you. I *am,* however, handing you your dragon on a proverbial silver platter. Surely Seth can wait?"

"No!" roared Maelstrom again, raising his sword and running towards the frozen form of Mediochre. "See how you like this! I am not a pawn!"

"Maelstrom!" snapped the tempomancer. It was so unlike him to shout that Maelstrom actually hesitated, and turned. The tempomancer was in exactly the same position as he had been. There was no evidence that he had just shouted. He wasn't even looking at Maelstrom; he was still engrossed in his own fingernail.

"What?" demanded Maelstrom.

The tempomancer clicked his fingers.

Duck! came Deep Ocean's mental scream, as she opened her mouth and spewed a tremendous jet of white-hot flame in Mediochre's direction. Mediochre ducked, grabbing his hat and covering his head with it.

The entire swarm of missile bees suddenly swooped upwards, having found an even greater source of heat to lock onto above them. One of them found its path blocked, without explanation, by a human head.

The metal insect caught Maelstrom in the face as it tried to curve upwards. The dragon-slayer's large hands flew to his nose and mouth as a spurt of red blood escaped between them. The kinetic energy of the projectile hurled him backwards, where he landed heavily on top of Mediochre.

The rest of the missile bees continued their arc until they met the white-hot jet of flame above them, at which point they were instantly incinerated into nothing.

Mediochre rolled with the blow of the large body that had hit him, so that its own momentum caused it to roll off of him. Deep Ocean cut off her flame and the room fell silent and dark, a glaring afterimage streaked across Mediochre's vision as he blinked repeatedly, trying to adjust to the sudden darkness again.

Just when he thought he had it clear, he felt something zip past his head, worryingly close to his right ear. He dodged to the side and turned to check whether Deep Ocean was OK.

The dragon gave an angry roar and tried to stand up, but stumbled, collapsing back onto her horde, her head crashing down onto the sharp crystals of quartz. A long, slim dart was protruding sickeningly from her right eye.

Mediochre spun around, scooping up his lighting charm and raising it above his head.

Joseph was down on one knee in the doorway, a black technomantic SSS night-vision rifle raised to his eye. Charlotte was kneeling next to him with her hands on her knees. And standing behind them, each hand pressing an ugly pistol to the back of a different head, was Mr Antler.

"Well done," Antler commented. "You didn't miss. Perhaps you get to live after all."

Joseph dropped Antler's tranquiliser rifle, seething silently, the firm, dangerous pressure of his own gun digging into the spot where his neck met his skull. He could see the look of panicked calculation – or possibly calculated panic – on Mediochre's face, lit from above by the glowing yellow charm.

"Then again," continued Antler's disembodied voice from behind him, "perhaps not." Joseph fought the urge to screw up his eyes, the all-too-familiar surge of terror that signified probable impending death wrenching at his insides.

"Antler, wait!" called Mediochre, urgently. "Think! Who fired those missile bees at me?" Joseph could imagine Antler's expression even though he could not see him: the slight sneer, the eyebrow raised in superiority.

"That, my dear dracologist, was a friend of mine," he scoffed. Joseph's mind raced; Antler was distracted, but not enough that he wouldn't notice if either Joseph or Charlotte moved. He glanced sideways at his fellow hostage. There was the hint of a tear in the corner of her eye, but she was fighting it back. She was biting her lower lip, and her hand was trembling slightly as it rested on her leg.

Brave girl, he thought approvingly. *I was a wreck the first time* I *was taken hostage.*

"Exactly," continued Mediochre, not moving from where he stood to ensure Antler didn't get nervous. "And where is that friend now?"

There was a pause. Joseph flicked his eyes in the other direction, to the spot at which Mediochre seemed to be staring. There was no-one there. There was, however, now that he looked harder, a slim trail of blood leading from a point beside Mediochre to the point where the missing SSS agent had presumably been, and a larger smear of blood on the wall.

"Someone large and wounded crashed into me and then ran over to your friend in all the commotion, probably angry at having just been shot," Mediochre explained. "I didn't see who it was, but I can work it out, because I'm the one who helped to wound him. And I reckon by now he's worked out that you guys have been playing him all along, and he's probably none too happy about it. So the question is: where is he now?"

Joseph felt the pressure on the back of his head weaken slightly as Antler stopped concentrating on him and started glancing around the cavern nervously. Very gently, he eased his head forward until the gun was not touching it, and then slowly moved it around to the side. He glanced at Charlotte beside him and nodded. Very carefully, she repeated the manoeuvre.

Joseph winked at her, then very quickly stood up, pivoting as he did so, and brought his fist smacking into Antler's face.

There was an unpleasant crunch, followed immediately by two gunshots as Antler's trigger-fingers reacted to his reflexes. Twin bullets disappeared into the darkness, imbedding themselves in the cavern floor. While Antler was still reeling from the broken nose, Joseph brought the side of his hand down hard on the larger man's left wrist, causing him to drop the gun, and then stepped back and kicked the other gun from his right hand. Charlotte yelped as it hit the wall and went off, and a cloud of dust was thrown up from the floor in front of her.

Joseph tried to hit Antler again, but a huge hand grabbed his fist and stopped it from getting any further. Antler's other hand slammed knuckle-first into Joseph's chest with a sound like a steak hitting a wooden slab. All the air was suddenly forced out of Joseph's lungs as Antler threw him, gasping, to the floor.

The SSS soldier aimed a furied kick at Joseph's side, but Joseph managed to roll with it, get a purchase on the rock below him with his foot, and then spring forwards, driving his right fist into Antler's groin. The large man doubled up, just as Joseph's other fist caught him in the throat with a powerful uppercut.

Antler flew into a berserker-like rage, flailing at Joseph unrelentingly with both fists. Joseph managed to dodge the first blow and block the second with his forearm, but even so the strength behind the blow made him stagger backwards, wincing. Antler came at him again, and Joseph ducked under an arm like a flailing iron girder and reached up, grabbing Antler's damaged nose and twisting it as hard as he could.

Antler screamed, the piercing sound making Charlotte wince, but a second later his huge paw of a hand caught Joseph on the side of the head and sent him reeling, his eyes seeming to actually spin in their sockets. The enraged Antler wrapped first one massive hand, and then another, around the front of Joseph's head, threatening to crush it like a nut in a nutcracker. Joseph's arms flailed desperately against his adversary's sides, but Antler ignored them.

Mediochre appeared at Charlotte's side as she prepared herself to join the conflict.

"Don't go in without a plan," he whispered. "Our intelligence is our only advantage against this guy."

"I take it you have a plan already?" she asked, following him as he quietly scurried up behind Antler.

"Not a very good one," Mediochre admitted. "But it'll do." He handed her one of the guns Antler had confiscated from Joseph, which Joseph had then disarmed from Antler. "Cudgel," he said simply. "Hit-and-run. Makes people angry. Angry people do stupid things."

With that, he removed his hat and leapt onto Antler's back, jamming the hat over his eyes and using it to pull his head back. Antler roared and let go of Joseph with one hand, ready to knock Mediochre away. Charlotte shrugged and brought the grip of the gun down hard on Antler's hip. The hand suddenly changed direction as she jumped backwards, heading for where she had been. She nipped around to Antler's other side and hit him in the side of the head.

With a frustrated scream, Antler let go of Joseph with the other hand and tore the hat from his head, casting it and Mediochre with it to the floor and rounding on Mediochre and Charlotte. He got no further, because at that point Joseph drove and angry elbow into the small of his back, followed by an equally angry chop to the neck, before spinning so that he brought the same elbow back into Antler's chest, bringing the fist of the same arm up so that the back of it crashed into his face, and then turning and bringing the other fist, hard, into Antler's temple.

As the man reeled from the onslaught, Joseph leant in and plucked the gun his opponent had been too angry to remember about from Antler's belt, clicked off the safety and pointed it at the smuggler's head.

"No," said Mediochre harshly. Joseph stopped and took a breath. The fury drained slowly from his face. He tucked the gun into his own belt and instead grabbed Antler at the point where his shoulder met his neck. After a few seconds the man went rigid, and eventually collapsed, unconscious, to the floor.

"A terribly useful technique, known to certain sci-fi fans as the Vulcan Sleeper Grip," Joseph commented as he walked over to join the other two. "Causes a build-up of blood in the head or something. He'll be out for a while, if I did it correctly. Now where's big-bad-evil-guy number two?"

Kurt Blackthorn winced as a fresh twang of pain shot through his torso. He was leaning against the rock face for support, both hands clamped over the relentlessly bleeding gash in his abdomen. Maelstrom's face leered at him out of the blur that had become of his vision.

"The theory is simple, really," the dragon-slayer explained. "We force Seth to choose between humans and monsters. If you're lucky, he chooses humans and you get a chance of survival. If not, you can know that you died proving to the world that Seth is a traitor to his species."

They were standing a few steps inside an opening half way up the cavern wall, which Maelstrom's keen hunter's eyes had happened to catch sight of when the cavern was lit up by the dragon's flame. It had taken them a while to find the route to it from the cavern, and another while to get there, as Maelstrom had had to carry Blackthorn almost the entire way, not having had the foresight to wait until they were up there before stabbing him.

Without warning, Maelstrom seized Blackthorn by the front of his uniform, dragged him over to the opening and shoved him off the edge, dangling him in the air with one hand.

"SETH!" Maelstrom roared, his deep voice echoing repeatedly off the cavern walls.

Far below, Mediochre looked up. He had calculated that Maelstrom would either return to the cavern to finish off Deep Ocean, or else would make himself known to them by some means, and so they had remained waiting where they were.

"Here are my terms, Seth!" bellowed Maelstrom from above. "You and your little group find your way up here within twenty minutes, or the boy is dropped. If any of you give up and I see you re-entering this cavern, he gets dropped anyway!"

Mediochre cursed. Joseph reached for his gun, but Mediochre waved at him to stop. If Maelstrom was shot it wouldn't kill him, but it would kill the hostage he was holding over a sizeable drop.

"What do we do?" asked Charlotte quietly. Mediochre glowered up at Maelstrom.

"We adhere to his terms," he whispered. "I find my way up to that opening, and nobody is seen re-entering this cavern."

"And the incredibly clever plan you've just thought of is..." Charlotte prompted.

"It's not incredibly clever," Mediochre said. "Just clever enough to outsmart him. And I'll explain that once we've left."

And with that, they ran from the cavern.

Mediochre ran through the underground passages and corridors carved from the rock by countless centuries of weathering. He could hear the footsteps of the other two behind him, but he paid no attention to them. Every so often he would come to an intersection where he had to stop and close his eyes, his fingers dancing over the keys of an imaginary piano, before running one way or the other.

He anxiously checked his watch. Over seventeen minutes gone already. He may not make it.

Maelstrom kept his eyes on the cavern below him for the full twenty minutes, making sure no-one came back in. When the time was up, he glanced back into the passage behind him. Blackthorn whimpered and trembled slightly in his hands.

There was the sound of frantic running. Maelstrom smiled. He waited, staring intently into the darkness. He drew his sword as the sound of running increased. It definitely sounded like three people, but he couldn't be sure...

The small, slight figure of Mediochre Q Seth emerged from the darkness, running towards him, calling his name. He waited for a few more seconds. Sure enough, two other figures could be made out in the gloom, running after Seth. They were all here.

Maelstrom shoved Blackthorn towards them, but Seth dodged past him and leapt at Maelstrom. The Blood Iron sword flashed and Seth recoiled. Maelstrom grinned, turned, and launched himself off the edge, into the darkness of the cavern below, hurling his sword away from himself to ensure he wouldn't land on it.

Teeth gritted, grasping his forearm, Mediochre took a short run-up and launched himself off after him.

The air rushed past Mediochre's face at astonishing speed as he fought to keep his head as high as possible, all four limbs outstretched in different directions in an attempt to maintain his position as he plummeted towards the hard rock below.

He knew that, as long as he didn't land head-first and turn his skull inside-out, he would heal from any damage caused by the fall. Even so, his eyes were screwed up as tightly shut as they would go, and his teeth were gritted so hard they threatened to break, in anticipation of the oncoming pain. A wordless scream escaped from behind them and was whipped away into his slipstream.

Oh God, prayed the one tiny part of his brain that wasn't screaming or thinking about the ground, *please let this work.*

There was a hideous sound, somewhere between a crunch and a squelch, as Maelstrom's fall was brought to a sudden, violent end. A second or so later, the world for Mediochre became one huge all-encompassing burst of unbearable agony.

Darkness reigned.

Mediochre's entire body spasmed, like a man awaking from a vivid nightmare, as his eyes snapped open, his lungs suddenly gasping in a huge amount of air as if checking to make sure they still could.

He could feel a thin layer of his own blood coating the inside of his clothes, but he knew that this meant that they had kept the rest of it in, along with its uncanny healing properties, which was why he was still here.

Slowly, carefully, he raised himself up on his arms and, only slightly impeded by sudden bursts of dizziness, got to his feet.

Several feet away from him, Maelstrom had also recovered, and was now retrieving his sword from where it had landed. Mediochre hurried towards him as fast as the unnatural darkness gathering at the corner of his vision would allow, but he knew that Maelstrom would undoubtedly reach Deep Ocean before him.

Mediochre's fumbling hands reached for his belt as Maelstrom stopped beside the mighty dragon's neck, turning, a look of cruel triumph on his face.

"I'm glad you're here to see this," he sneered, raising the sword as Mediochre desperately tried to cover the last few feet between them.

The sword began to fall. With a final tug, Mediochre pulled the belt from around his waist and, with a deft flick of the wrist, sent the metal buckle snapping into Maelstrom's hand.

Maelstrom gave a short gasp of pain and surprise, and his grip on the sword weakened involuntarily. With another flick, Mediochre wrapped the belt around the blade and tugged it from the hunter's hand. He shook his head to clear it and allowed himself a brief cocky grin.

"What do you know," he smiled as Maelstrom stared dumbly at his suddenly-empty hand. "It *is* all in the wrist."

Maelstrom glared at him, a glare full of 350 years of unadulterated hatred. He yanked a long hunting knife from his own belt and pointed it threateningly at Mediochre.

"OK Seth," he hissed. "OK. Let's settle this whole thing between us now then, shall we? Think about it, Seth. What chance do you think you have of defeating me?"

"Scale of one to ten?" asked Mediochre. "About... Tuesday."

"What?" spat Maelstrom, as if he couldn't believe his adversary's stupidity. Mediochre merely smiled.

Having heard Mediochre's code word, Joseph Carrion vaulted over Deep Ocean's neck, gun in hand, and landed beside Maelstrom, pointing the weapon at his head. At the same instant, Charlotte emerged around the dragon's head, pointing his other gun at the other side of Maelstrom's head with the inexperienced aim of someone who's never used a firearm but is close enough to the target that it doesn't matter.

Mediochre reached behind him and drew the gun Joseph had taken from Antler, pointing it at Maelstrom's chest.

"Confuse the enemy," he said happily. "Rule number twelve of gaining the upper hand."

Maelstrom stared, uncomprehendingly, first at Joseph, than at Charlotte, and then up to the opening high above where he had recently been.

Two of Kurt Blackthorn's comrades, dressed in their SSS uniforms, were sitting, dangling their legs off the edge, watching them. One of them waved.

"Ah yes," said Mediochre. "Those are my new friends, Oscar and Stephanie. I managed to convince them to stand in as decoys and still have time enough to reach you, isn't that impressive? Mind you, since their choice was not-getting-the-egg-back-but-helping-save-their-friend or not-geting-the-egg-back-and-staying-behind-to-continue-being-beaten-up-by-a-Dhampir, I'd say the results were fairly easy to predict."

Maelstrom dropped his knife, almost graciously.

"Well," he said, quietly. "It appears that's it then. I have been vanquished. Mind you," he went on, leaning back against the scaly neck behind him, "I'm not sure that one could call this defeat. After all, I've killed perhaps over three hundred dragons without you stopping me. That gives us the final score of 300-1. I don't know about here, but in my country that still constitutes victory."

"Shut up," snarled Mediochre, his eyes hardening, his grip tightening on the weapon. Charlotte glanced nervously at Joseph, who shrugged helplessly. Maelstrom leaned in closer to Mediochre and continued in a conspiratorial whisper.

"Remember the last time we met like this?" he asked. "Me trying to destroy a monster, you trying to save it? Didn't work out quite the same that time, did it. What's it like, knowing that you'll have to carry the memory of that failure for your entire life? And a long, long life at that..."

"Maelstrom, shut *up*," snapped Mediochre again.

"Do as he says you piece of filth!" hissed Joseph, kicking Maelstrom on the shin.

"Very well, very well," said Maelstrom, leaning back again. "I'll come quietly. I can settle for a lifetime score of three hundred. Although –"

Without warning, Maelstrom flicked his foot behind himself and kicked two items into the air. One was his hunting knife. The other flashed blue in the light from Joseph's charm as Maelstrom caught them both, one in each hand.

"I'd prefer three hundred and one," Maelstrom finished.

There was a deafening boom and Maelstrom's body was thrown back hard against

Deep Ocean's neck. Glint the egg fell to the ground at his feet, unharmed. Maelstrom gasped, staring disbelievingly at Mediochre. The fresh red hole in the middle of his chest remained for a few seconds, before it started to shrink.

Mediochre fired again. And again. Maelstrom's body jerked with each new gunshot, Mediochre's unseeing eyes staring at him, watching the grotesque dance. Joseph was screaming Mediochre's name over and over. Charlotte had already dropped the gun she'd been holding and was backing away in horror.

Eventually, Mediochre realised that the gun was no longer firing, an in place of the thunderous, echoing booming there was only a series of sharp clicks. He turned to Joseph.

"Give me another gun," he said. Joseph stared into his friend's eyes, eyes that had taken on a coldness they had never had before. "Give me another gun!" Mediochre repeated, louder. Joseph hit him.

It was a good punch. Mediochre's unconscious form half-rolled, half-tumbled down the slope of quartz. Maelstrom slid down Deep Ocean's neck, leaving an ugly red smear against the blue scales. His chest had been literally blown open, and his eyes showed no signs of life. Joseph knelt in front of him and felt for a pulse.

"Come on," he whispered, more to himself than to Maelstrom. "Your magic blood can't already be past its expiry date. Heal, dammit. Come on. I can't give CPR to someone who doesn't *have* a chest. Heal. Heal, you son of a... *Heal*!"

Nothing. Charlotte took a deep breath, turned around and threw up.

Dhampinella was actually panting heavily as she punched an SSS soldier between the eyes, drove her elbow sideways into the head of another, turned to chop a third in the back of the neck as he ran past her, and ran two steps to the left to claw at the face of a fourth.

After Mediochre had arrived and convinced two of them to come with him unarmed, most of the others had lost morale and fled. Of those that hadn't, all were tired and bruised and none had any working weapons left. But that didn't mean much when Dhampinella herself could no longer see straight and was struggling to breathe.

Eventually she stopped, her breath coming in ragged gasps. Her arms hung limp at her sides; she was too exhausted to even raise them. Her copper-coloured hair was slick with sweat.

The ground all around her was littered with unconscious humans. There were a few further away that were now conscious again but who were not entirely sure whether they were humans as opposed to, for example, bunny rabbits.

The only SSS thug who was still standing was a short distance away from Dhampinella. She couldn't make out, through her own haze of fatigue, what the soldier looked like, or even their gender. She could tell it was humanoid, and her sixth sense told her it was fully alive, but apart from that she couldn't make *anything* out.

The soldier raised their arm. They appeared to be holding something. Most likely they had found a working weapon. Just what she needed.

She forced herself to reach up and wipe the sweat out of her eyes. She blinked several times and shook her head in an attempt to clear it. She looked back at the soldier, prepared to throw herself to one side if they fired.

And then she became aware of another living thing behind it, and a whole host of others not far away.

The thug dropped their weapon and pitched forwards, felled from behind by someone holding what appeared to be a tree branch.

"Hélène?" Dhampinella asked muzzily as her rescuer came closer. Then, like a felled tree, she toppled slowly forwards into the French girl's arms.

From her vantage point leaning on Hélène's shoulder, Dhampinella could now see the other approaching life signs: a small army of MIPF officers in riot gear were marching in formation towards them.

"Couldn't you have arrived earlier?" Dhampinella heard Hélène's voice yelling, as she drifted into an exhausted sleep.

Mediochre was in darkness. Blissful, restful, comfortable darkness. Faint pictures floated lazily through his mind: images of blind old ladies and blonde young girls and glittering eggs and magnificent dragons. Images of muscle-bound smugglers and snarling dogs and crazed hunters. Images of –

The darkness suddenly parted to reveal a real image, slightly blurred, which eventually focussed itself and became the stern face of a late-middle-aged, silver-haired man of Greek origin, wearing a crisp white shirt with rolled-up sleeves and three pens of different colours sticking out of the breast pocket. He was flanked by two figures wearing the standard green uniform of a medimancer.

"Dr Modern?" Mediochre hazarded.

"Ah, you are awake," replied Dr Prometheus Modern, an old acquaintance of Mediochre and Joseph and a man who could do unbelievable things with nothing more to work with than a kitchen knife, some slightly rusted tweezers, a bottle of Schnapps and a length of wool. And had had to, on more than one occasion, when Joseph had got into some particularly nasty fights.

Dr Modern scratched his beard and walked off, muttering to himself in Greek, while Mediochre sat up, the sleepiness slowly draining from his mind. Satisfied that he was OK, the medimancers left the room purposefully.

He inspected his right forearm. Sure enough, the cut from the Blood Iron sword was clearly visible as a thin, horizontal red line running across it. The flesh was held together with several black stitches, and Mediochre could even recognise Modern's expert needlework. It was ironic, in an odd way, to have survived for 350 years without ever acquiring a wound that lasted more than a minute or so and yet to now have a forearm that would never be healed. He wondered vaguely who was going to have to restitch it every time the stitches decomposed.

"How are the others?" Mediochre called out to Dr Modern, who was now scanning the top sheet of a sheaf of notes through his half-moon reading glasses.

"Joseph and girl are both right as rain and on their feet," replied the doctor, glancing up at him. "Dhampir woman is healthy but drowsy, after sleeping for a long time. French woman is OK. Mouse is remarkably unharmed, worse luck." He glanced over at a thick-walled glass tank on a small table beside the sterile hospital bed in which Mediochre lay, inside which Desra snuffled happily at the glass.

She was not allowed out of this enclosure whenever she was with Dr Modern, Mediochre remembered, ever since an unfortunate accident involving a lab rat that had been genetically-engineered through use of experimental mancy. Mediochre smiled at the memory as Prometheus continued.

"Most of soldiers in stable condition with minor fractures, mild laceration and excessive bruising. Six hospitalised with concussion. Chief smuggler stable but angry. Stab victim stable, but with larger version of wound like yours – no organ damage luckily. Slayer man has nasty case of D.O.A."

"Oh no," moaned Mediochre, placing his head in his hands, as he remembered his actions shortly before he was knocked out.

"I would not worry," said Modern, removing the top sheet and placing it at the bottom of the sheaf, before studying the next one. "According to his age, he should already be dead. According to his records, he *is* already dead. Killing of dead people is not illegal. Possibly not even immoral." He suddenly looked up at Mediochre. "Oh yes," he added. "I forgot. Now that you're awake, politician wants to see you. He seems very angry."

"Ah," responded Mediochre, running a hand through his hair.

Sure enough, MAB MP James Chrome was standing in the foyer of the hospital, flanked by a dozen or so of the MIPF officers who, Mediochre assumed, were responsible for getting himself and everyone else here.

Joseph and Charlotte were already standing with him, very deliberately not looking at him. Dhampinella was sitting poker-straight in a metal chair beside them. Both the bullet-wound in Joseph's hand and the one in Dhampinella's arm appeared to have been repaired.

"Hello, Dr Seth," said Chrome in meticulously measured tones. His facial expression was not quite so controlled.

"Jim," Mediochre replied, nodding in greeting.

"You are to come with me," Chrome stated. "The PM wants a word with you. Several words, in fact. And I wouldn't mind a few myself."

"How about alabandical and spanghew?" Mediochre suggested. "As words go, I'm quite fond of those two." Chrome glowered.

"I am not in the mood for humour, Dr Seth. Come. Now."

At the Scottish MABGov Headquarters, Mediochre was ushered through a set of heavy-looking mahogany doors into a private meeting chamber while the other three were made to sit outside. There were already several important people seated around the central table, and Chrome took his place between the Chief of the Edinburgh MIPF and the head of the Royal Society for Dracology.

At the head of the table was a middle-aged woman in an expensive grey trouser suit, her light-brown hair tied back, looking at Mediochre through the lenses of her spectacles like a teacher looking at a particularly disorganised child.

"Prime Minister!" exclaimed Mediochre jovially, spreading his arms. "Queen MAB! Kathryn! Kaz! Kitty-kat! Ka-wa!" the MAB Prime Minister narrowed her eyebrows slightly.

"The line comes just after Kaz, Mediochre. I'd appreciate it if you didn't cross it again."

"Sorry, Miss Prime Ministerness Sir," said Mediochre, sitting down. Queen MAB did not respond.

"I'm assured, Dr Seth," she said once he was seated, "that you and your friends can technically be arrested right now for numerous crimes including theft of government equipment, assault of governmental officers, endangering lives through negligence in the course of duty, attempt to reveal MABGov secrets to the Mantically Unaware, and several counts of generally disturbing the peace." She checked the notes in front of her. "And, it appears, unauthorised entry to a restricted area of a National Park. Have you anything to say for yourself?"

Mediochre bit his lip in exaggerated thought, twirled a pencil between his fingers for a while, and whistled the first few bars of *Little Spanish Flea* before answering.

"Only that had I not, an incredibly rare example of a dragon-only genetic trait would be gone, an innocent and intelligent dragon would be dead, and the Scottish branch of the SSS would still be at large." He turned to the head of the Royal Society for Dracology, a small grey-haired woman named Mary MacDonald. "How is Deep Ocean, by the way? And Glint?"

"I believe the dragon and her egg are unharmed and recovering well," replied Mary, her frail hands clasped on the table in front of her. "I am also told that she telepathically expressed her wishes that you be personally thanked by the Society. We cannot deny that without you, she would not have survived." Mediochre smiled and thanked her.

"This is irrelevant!" snapped Chrome irritably, and the MIPF chief beside him nodded his consent. "You still have not given us enough reason to let you go free!"

"Indeed," agreed the MIPF chief, whose name, Mediochre vaguely remembered, was Steven. "I lost several good officers in the Sapphire Storage fiasco. That's human blood on your hands, Seth." Mediochre narrowed his eyes.

"Nothing to do with me, Steve," he replied, and noted from the look on the man's face that evidently his name was not Steven after all. "My operations in there were entirely my own and did not involve your officers in any way. Both the firefight and the explosion took place while I was absent, for reasons of which I am unaware, although I can hazard a guess. And a large part of that guess is that your operation was badly organised, badly planned and badly executed. The MIPF officers whom I saw in that facility were not the highly-trained, well-commanded officers that arrived in the Cairngorms or escorted Jimmy here to the hospital. I don't know who was in charge of that mission or what the officers' briefing said, but I do know that even my inexperienced cousin could see that it could have been better handled, and he died 370 years ago."

"You stole my helicopter!" snapped Chrome, pointing an accusing finger, as the man whose name was not Steve stared at Mediochre open-mouthed in shock and anger. Mediochre leaned back and steepled his fingers.

"Only after you deliberately attempted to pervert the course of a crucial operation at a critical point," he pointed out. "And I could perhaps also note that this was at the time when you should have been worrying about the fact that a badly-concealed smuggler cell which had been trading from a port under your jurisdiction for years without you noticing had just blown up and taken a sizeable chunk of the street with it. Some people might, at this point, use the term 'priority list'."

Chrome jumped up from his chair and was about to shout something at Mediochre when he was cut off by Queen MAB's sharp voice.

"Sit *down* Mr Chrome!" she barked. Chrome sat. "The man is right. Your conduct in recent times has been questionable to say the least. I'm aware that the same can be said of Dr Seth, however, it would be prudent to remember that he is a slayer-catcher and a field dracologist, a man for whom split-second decisions are a necessary part of his occupation. You, on the contrary, are a government minister, and you should be concentrating on making sure all your decisions are the most beneficial for your country and its people. You should *not* be concentrating on petty authority feuds with respected members of the education system!"

"I take it you mean me there?" interrupted Mediochre. Queen MAB flashed him a warning glare. "Just checking," he said quietly.

"A full investigation into the matters raised will, I'm sure, begin forthwith," Queen MAB continued. "Which, I believe, brings this meeting to a close unless anyone else has any issues they wish to raise."

There followed a half-hour or so of political bickering which, for the most part, Mediochre spent sketching a still-life of Desra sniffing at a pencil.

After a while, the MIPF officers left the room outside the meeting room to go and guard the entrance hall, leaving Joseph, Charlotte and Dhampinella alone. Dhampinella appeared to have dozed off again, leaning against a stone pillar with her eyes closed, appearing for all the world like a very detailed sculpture.

"Is he going to be arrested?" Charlotte asked. "Or worse?" Joseph shook his head.

"Mediochre's talked his way out of worse situations than this before," he assured her. "He has a unique way of playing politicians and other legal-type people. Oh, and he went to school with Queen MAB, which also helps." Charlotte was unconvinced.

"But... he killed Maelstrom," she protested. "He wouldn't let you kill Antler, and then he killed Maelstrom. Isn't that just slightly illegal, not to mention hypocritical?" Joseph laughed.

"They can't arrest him for killing someone who's already been declared dead, even if it wasn't in the course of stopping him from killing Glint. Killing one of the more sentient species of dragon is classified as murder."

"It's still hypocrisy," Charlotte argued. Joseph shook his head.

"Nah," he said. "It's just Mediochrisy." Charlotte raised an eyebrow.

"The difference being...?"

"That it's done by Mediochre," explained Joseph. Charlotte was shocked.

"But that's terrible!" she gasped.

"Nope," replied Joseph, leaning back in his chair and putting his hands behind his head. "It's mediocre." Charlotte rolled her eyes.

"I think we've had enough puns on his name," she said. Joseph smiled.

"Look," he said. "Mediochre's one of the leading experts on dracology in the world. He's stopped more catastrophes than you've had maths lessons. He's served as the MABGov's moral compass on pretty much every occasion they've had a big decision to make. He's saved my life so many times I've lost count - the guy once fought off a skeletal horde with his teeth while trying to get my own unconscious form to safety. I'm not saying that gives him any more rights than other people, but... well... sometimes you can overlook someone's mistakes based on how rare it is for them to actually make one."

The door to the entrance hall opened and a bored-sounding voice announced:

"Some visitor wants to see Miss Johnson." Charlotte looked up and emitted a sudden gasp of delight.

Danny Snapfax strolled into the room, grinning, in a smart grey business suit. The bored guard outside closed the door again as soon as Danny was in. He spread his arms and walked towards Charlotte.

Without warning, Joseph stood up abruptly, pulling a gun from inside his shirt and pointing it at Danny's face. Charlotte stared in open-mouthed horror, too shocked even to say anything.

"Come a single step closer and I will perform an intrusive anatomical examination of your interior structure using a bullet where I normally use a scalpel," announced Joseph. Danny stopped, appearing taken aback for a moment. Then he smiled, like a man who has just got a joke.

"But Dr Carrion," he protested innocently, "I fall outside of your realm of study, being very much alive." Joseph didn't return the smile.

"You're very much alive *right now*," he corrected. Danny's grin wavered, and then died.

"What are you doing?" screamed Charlotte, finally finding her tongue. Joseph didn't turn to look at her, keeping his eyes trained on his target.

"I'm sure he's a very charming person and everything," he answered, "but I doubt he could convince a warehouse-load of angry smugglers to let him walk out safely. And I was in the same hospital as some of the people who got hit by that explosion. In general, they don't look very good right now. And that's just the people who were on the fringes. You were down in the bowels of the storage facility when we left you. Almost at ground zero. I watched the news on the hospital ward TV. No-one who was in that part of the building escaped unscathed. And here you are, not a mark on you."

"I managed to escape before the explosion," Danny said, raising his hands in a surrendering gesture. Joseph narrowed his eyes.

"Not unless you can freeze time you didn't," he said quietly. "You don't need Mediochre's skill to work out that, even when he wasn't being attacked at the time, a human being couldn't have escaped that place that quickly. Unless he happened to have a friend who *could* stop time."

"Joseph –" Danny began, but Joseph ignored him.

"There was only one tempomancer in that building," he continued. "And he's the one you told Charlotte you weren't friends with any more. I don't like people who lie to the people who trust them."

Danny said nothing. Charlotte's mind was reeling; she didn't know what to think. She looked into the beautiful blue eyes that, until recently, she hadn't thought she would ever see again. Danny *couldn't* be lying. He *wouldn't*. There had to be some other explanation. But how could she tell?

"Danny?" she asked. Danny swallowed slightly.

"Charlotte?"

"How did you know where the tempomancer was? Didn't he check after he betrayed your organisation that no-one was following him?"

"They... they're better at following people than he thought," explained Danny, his voice wavering with fear.

"And how did you know the inside of the Triple-S building so well?"

"We... came across blueprints."

"And if it was so important that you caught the tempomancer, why did you run away before the explosion?"

"I was chasing him."

"And why weren't you still chasing him when he arrived in the Cairngorms?"

"He lost me."

"But aren't your people better at following people than he realised?"

"He's... a quick learner."

"Why aren't you still after him?"

"They gave that task to someone else."

"Who?"

"I'm sorry?"

"Who's in your organisation? Who are they? You can tell us, we won't spread it around. This room doesn't even have any cameras in it. It's safe. If your organisation really is doing good, tell us who they are. Please."

"I..."

"Please, Danny."

Danny looked at her helplessly for a few moments, before his face crumpled and his entire posture seemed to sag.

"I think," said Joseph slowly, "that you should leave. If you do it now, I won't tell the men outside to arrest you until you're gone."

"Charlotte –" Danny began, but he was cut off by the click of a safety catch being released.

"I don't want to have to hurt you in front of Charlotte, Danny," he said. "Please. Leave."

Danny hesitated for a moment more, before turning around and walking casually through the door, closing it behind himself.

"Was that a good idea?" asked Dhampinella's voice from behind them. Joseph turned. The Dhampir was still leaning against the pillar, but her eyes were open.

"In the country in which I was born, there was a special word for people who do what he's done," she continued.

"Dhampinella, were you awake for *all* of that?" Joseph asked, bewildered. His apprentice shrugged.

"I was ready to hit him if he said no," she said.

Charlotte, however, was not paying attention to them. Walking slowly, she left the room, passed through the guards beyond, who deemed her not dangerous enough to bother about, and out into the street.

She sat down on the edge of the kerb, staring blankly at the road. She felt it when the first tears began to weave their way down her skin, but she did nothing to wipe them away.

Charlotte did not know how long she had been sitting there when someone sat next to her and placed a comforting arm on her shoulder. She turned her head to see whoever it was.

As it happened, it was Mediochre. He looked at her sadly, and then gave a quiet sigh.

"I wish there was something I could say that would make it better," he said. "There isn't, though. There never is. But I know how you feel." He hesitated, looking at her more closely. "Maybe not exactly how you feel. I can guess though. He had us all fooled. Even me. And I'd known him for longer than the rest of you."

He looked up, apparently lost in thought. "I was a bit of an idiot on that count, to be honest. I ought to have noticed there was something up before now. The curse of hindsight, I suppose. There's a reason why the Ancient Greeks named a monstrous Titan after it."[3]

It was getting dark now. Charlotte had lost all track of time since they had first set off to return Glint to his mother. She had no idea whether or not this was the same day. She couldn't even have said for sure if it was the same week.

Mediochre sighed again. "A very clever person once told me it was better to have loved and lost than never to have loved at all. He was wrong, of course. I've known people who've never loved at

---

[3]   This may not be true, but there is a Titan named Epimetheus, which roughly translates as 'hindsight'. Give the guy a little credit.

all, and they're usually happy enough. Loving and losing though..." He closed his eyes for a moment, breathing out. "It isn't fun. But it will get easier in time. It always gets easier in time." He thoughtfully ran a finger down the stitching on his arm. "Time heals everything, if only you have enough of it," he said sadly, as much to himself as to Charlotte. "But, like I say, I know this doesn't help."

He looked suddenly so downcast, even compared to her, that Charlotte touched his arm gently. Mediochre looked at her, and she managed a weak smile.

"It does," she assured him. "A little." Mediochre smiled back, slightly less weakly. He reached into the depths of his pockets and, after a few false starts including Desra, a playing card and a toothbrush, he eventually produced a small blue scale that shimmered gently, even in the fast-fading light of dusk.

"A little present from Deep Ocean," he said. "Dragons shed their scales every few months to several years, depending on species and size. She felt it would be a fitting reminder of our time with Glint."

Charlotte took the scale and smiled again, with more genuine happiness than she had done before. Mediochre continued to look at her for a few moments, then swallowed slightly and looked away.

The entrance door to the MABGov HQ opened, and Queen MAB walked out, with James Chrome just behind her and Joseph and Dhampinella behind him.

"One more thing before you leave, Dr Seth," she said. Mediochre turned and looked up.

"The girl," said Chrome, gesturing at Charlotte. "Who is she?" Mediochre stood up and brushed himself down.

"She," he replied, "is Charlotte Johnson, who is quite possibly the most brilliant person of her age in the country. She's also my new apprentice."

Chrome's mouth fell open and his eyes threatened to pop out of their sockets. Behind Mediochre, Charlotte gave a similar reaction, if less extreme. Queen MAB merely nodded.

"Very well," she said. "I expect the necessary paperwork within a month, as per the usual. I'm sure many people will be greatly interested by this news." She took a step forwards and leant down until she was at Mediochre's ear level. "By the way," she continued, "you're running out of favours I owe you. You might want to tread lightly for a while."

"I will certainly consider it," Mediochre said quietly. Queen MAB smiled.

"Night Sam," she whispered, straightening up. Mediochre winked.

"Night Ralph," he replied. Queen MAB tugged firmly at Chrome's sleeve.

"Do stop gawping like that, Chrome," she tutted. "It does not become you. Come on."

Mediochre watched them leave. The expression on his face was unreadable. At least, it was unreadable to anyone who hadn't known him all their life.

"You're thinking about Maelstrom, aren't you?" whispered Joseph, placing a hand lightly on his shoulder. Mediochre sighed slightly, and nodded.

"I could have stopped after the first shot," he said in a low, hushed tone. "Then he would have healed."

"No you couldn't have," insisted Joseph. "Nobody, put in your situation, facing that man, knowing what you knew, would have been able to stop after the first shot. Trust me."

"Even so..." Mediochre tailed off. Joseph sighed.

"I forgive you, Mediochre," he said. "The MABGov forgives you." he reached down and pulled at a small metal chain around Mediochre's neck, hidden by the collar of his shirt. A small metal cross dangled on the end. "He forgives you," finished Joseph, even more quietly. "What more do you need?"

He replaced the cross and chain, tucking it safely away so that Dhampinella couldn't see it, as it had been for as long as Joseph could remember. He turned around.

"Well," he said so that everyone could hear. "It's starting to get late. Time to go home?" Mediochre shook his head, almost as if clearing it.

"Nope," he said. "There's still something I need to do first. We'll get your car from Rowan and then I need you to take me to the University."

One bus ride, a short walk, an exchange of stories with Melinda and a car journey later, Mediochre walked into the office of Professor Kiwi Mashuga, Dean of St Merlin's University.

"Red!" she greeted him, in a tone of pleasant surprise. Mediochre closed the door behind him. "Finished your adventure already?" Mediochre looked at her sadly.

"Not quite," he said. Kiwi gave a mock frown.

"Not quite getting your drift here, I'm afraid. Not quite on the same sheet of paper. Not even on a photocopy. Sorry." Mediochre sighed, as Kiwi picked up her IMP from her desk and began tapping at the keypad.

"I've worked it out, Kiwi," he said. "I've worked out how the pyromancer got in here without our security doing anything."

"Do tell," said Kiwi, looking up and putting down the IMP.

"You let her in," said Mediochre simply. "She wouldn't need any technomantic expertise to shut down the security systems then. As Dean of the University, you can override them all. You told me that half the SSS kept you informed on who was trying to bring them down. I assumed it was a joke. I didn't even think at the time that the best way to throw my suspicion would be to do just that: accuse yourself in a non-serious manner. It implies you don't even take the subject seriously. It also means that the concept of you being the real culprit becomes too obvious to be true – you used the same logic with the Sapphire Storage Company's name. And the fact that your own University was attacked makes people see you as a victim, not a suspect."

"But Red," Kiwi protested, "she said herself that nobody in the university worked for the SSS."

"Indeed she did," agreed Mediochre. "And indeed they don't. But we never thought to turn that question on its head, did we? It's not that you work for the SSS. It's that the SSS work for you. That's the real reason why you knew so much about my case. That's the real reason why the SSS knew my movements so well. They and I were both working for the same person."

"You must be joking, surely?" Kiwi asked. Mediochre shook his head.

"I wish I was," he said. "But it's true. I just didn't work it out until I had a conversation with a dragon about being named after colours."

"What?" asked Kiwi, appearing confused.

"I used Chips to check the Duluxe colour chart on the way over here. Kiwi's a shade of green, while Sapphire is a shade of blue. Blue, red and green are the three primary colours of light. Everyone's heard the rumours that the entire SSS is run by just one person, a mysterious individual named Sapphire. You knew that I'd be coming after you soon enough, so you chose a code name that subtly referenced both your real name and your nickname for me. It was like your own personal in-joke."

"Red," Kiwi laughed, "this is hardly what you'd call definitive proof."

"No," conceded Mediochre, "but slightly more definitive is the fact that the SSS managed to get their hands on not one, not two, but *three* missile bee launchers. I checked that as well. No missile bee launchers have been reported stolen or missing anywhere in this country, without subsequently being returned, ever. But the Uni security team downstairs, when I asked them to check, had exactly the number it says they have on the documents. Which wouldn't be so odd if I hadn't pointed out to you when we got them that we were three over what we'd ordered. Remember that? You said you'd fix it, so I left it to you. Turns out you'd ordered an extra three for a reason."

Kiwi sighed, and leant against her desk.

"So," she said. "Are you going to do anything, or did you just come here to boast your awesome cleverness?"

"Actually," said Mediochre, "I just wanted to ask you why. I mean, not why you did the whole smuggling scene; that was obviously for money. But why did you let that young woman come in here after me and get taken down?"

"I thought you said that was to throw suspicion?"

"Yes. It was. But why *her*? Because that wasn't just any old SSS agent. I checked that as well. I've done a lot of checking this evening. You see, I had to go to the house of an old informant of mine to get the car that drove me here. And while I was there, she happened to mention that a contact of hers in the MIPF had told her some very interesting test results. They analysed the DNA of Miss Isobel Williams, and they found out which family she comes from."

He removed from his pocket a small scrap of paper, on which was drawn a rough sketch of a Bloodline Crest. He cleared away a pile of unfinished paperwork and held it up to the crest inlaid onto the top of Kiwi's desk.

"She was your own *daughter,* Kiwi," he said. Kiwi shrugged, evidently not seeing any reason to fuss.

"She was the most convenient person to use for the more secret of my operations," she explained. "When she turned up at the university, I thought, why not? It could be a good opportunity to, as you say, throw suspicion, not to mention distance myself from her if she was found out."

"You saw your own daughter as a *convenient person to use*?" Mediochre repeated.

"I'm sorry, Kiwi. Dean Mashuga. Sapphire. You're not the person I thought you were. You're definitely not the person I would once have given a second chance to."

Kiwi sighed, and thrust her hand at Mediochre, snapping her fingers as she did so. The air between them burst into flames, the jet of fire blasting him across the room and into the wall.

"That girl learned from the master," she commented dryly, as she reached into her robe with the other hand and removed a length of thick wire. "And you're right. I'm not the person you thought I was. I'm not nearly so soft. Or so stupid. The doors are already locked, and the CCTV's been deactivated." She cut off her flame and gestured to the IMP on her desk, which she had been tapping at earlier. "You might have healed from the burns Isobel gave you, but I'm sure you can still asphyxiate."

"Kiwi?" said Mediochre, mentally rolling his eyes at the panto-villain monologue he'd just heard. Kiwi ignored him, kneeling down and placing the cord over his throat. "Kiwi?" he repeated, more urgently, as she started to press down, cutting off his airway. Again she ignored him.

"Kiwi!" he tried to shout once more, although it came out as more of a croak. His hands flew to the cord and tried to drag it from his neck, but the Dean was stronger than him. Most people were.

"I've won!" he managed to cough. "I've tricked you, you fool!"

Kiwi stopped, her eyes narrowing, an expression of incomprehension on her face.

"What?" she asked, releasing the pressure on the cord. Mediochre sucked in a sudden rush of air, before heaving a sigh.

"You made me ruin it, you moron," he grumbled. "It was gonna be so good, like one of those smug moments in a film. You were gonna say 'what' and I was gonna... look, let's try that again: Kiwi?"

"What?!" asked Kiwi, angrily.

"The CCTV's still on."

"WHAT?"

Mediochre reached into his pocket and pulled out Chips the IMP, holding it so that Kiwi could clearly see the writing on the screen: 'Blocking All Frequencies'.

"I realise this makes me sound like my biological age," said Mediochre, "but my IMP's better than your IMP."

The door burst open so violently it tore one of its own hinges from the wall, and an entire phalanx of security guards marched in. Many were wearing looks of angered betrayal, which was probably fair enough in the circumstances. Most were also carrying weapons.

"I believe you've already met the Merlin U security team," said Mediochre, allowing himself a vengeful smile. "I think you may not be quite the person they thought you were either."

Mediochre walked through the university entrance doors into the car park outside. Charlotte was waiting for him in the cold air, Joseph having said his goodbyes and returned to his room and Dhampinella having gone off to wherever it was she actually slept at night, which not even Joseph actually knew.

"That's another favour or two Kathryn owes me," he said. "She's going to be *really* angry when she finds out what the Dean she paid was doing with her money's help." He smiled as Charlotte tried, and failed, to stifle a yawn.

"It really *is* late now," he said. "Come on, I'll drive you home. Nobody'll notice my apparent age in the dark. And my feet *do* actually still touch the pedals. Just about."

He led her over to a car which, although it was not registered in his name, he used whenever his work required him to drive somewhere. Charlotte was too tired to argue even if she wanted to.

She also did want to get home quite badly. She had just realised she was still wearing her school uniform.

Mr and Mrs Johnson were surprised when they arrived, although not as much as Mediochre would have expected. The reason for their surprise became immediately clear, as did the mystery of how Joseph had explained Charlotte's disappearance, when they found that a girl who looked exactly like Charlotte was asleep upstairs, having fallen ill.

A brief examination by Mediochre confirmed that what they had upstairs was actually something he referred to as an 'Avatar' – a sort of solid mantic illusion of a human being that was, to the untrained eye, indistinguishable from a real human apart from the fact that it could only perform a few simple actions which it would be 'pre-programmed' with beforehand. Something like, for example, 'enter house; claim you're unwell; walk to bedroom; pretend to sleep'.

"It seems I'm not the only one with some very clever contacts," Mediochre noted, after getting Charlotte to tap the Avatar twice on the forehead and thus causing it to fade away. "These things are hard to make. They must have used footage from the security cameras at St Merlin's to get your looks right. I must ask Joseph who did it."

In the hour or so that followed, Mediochre and Charlotte explained to her parents everything that had happened to their daughter since they had last seen her for real. They seemed disapproving, as would be expected, but they both agreed that, since it was what she'd wanted and she hadn't actually been hurt, there was no harm done. Mediochre whispered to Charlotte that this was probably only because they were in shock after learning that magic was real, but that he wasn't going to argue. When they had finished talking, Charlotte took Mediochre aside.

"Did you mean what you said about making me your apprentice?" she asked. Mediochre looked unsure, and slightly sheepish.

"Well, actually, I only said that because an apprentice is one of the few Mantically-Unaware people you're allowed to reveal the existence of mancy to under MAB law. If I hadn't said something I'd have been arrested and you'd have had your memory erased. It was that or claim you were my wife."

"Oh," said Charlotte, slightly dejected. Mediochre looked for a second as if he was about to reach out to her, then decided against it and put his hand behind his back.

"That... doesn't necessarily mean I won't consider teaching you for real," he said "If you want. And your parents agree."

"Really?" asked Charlotte. Mediochre looked oddly grim.

"I'll think about it," he replied. "But for now, I'd better be getting home."

"You can stay overnight if you want," Charlotte said, glancing at her parents, who shrugged. "We've got a spare room. It's a bit late to be driving across the city."

Mediochre dithered for a while, but eventually accepted. It *had* been a while since he'd last slept, unless you counted time spent unconscious as sleep, and he knew the dangers of driving while tired well enough.

Checking Desra was OK, he made his way upstairs to the room he'd been directed to, removed his hat and body-warmer, and fell onto the bed. His eyes stared at a spot on the wall, painted in the bland, neutral tones of spare bedrooms worldwide, as he briefly considered his next move. Then, finally, his exhausted teenage body forced him to sleep.

Charlotte awoke at some point in the mid-morning and took a few seconds to verify that everything that had happened to her recently had indeed happened, rather than just being some excessively bizarre dream.

Once she had washed and dressed, she decided that there was only one way she could be entirely sure either way, so she walked up to the door of the spare bedroom and knocked quietly.

When there was no answer, she knocked louder. And louder.

Eventually, she gently pushed open the door. There was no-one there. The room was empty, the bed was pristinely made. The window... was open.

Oh no. He wouldn't have. Would he? Quite apart from the fact it was considered rude to leave without saying goodbye, they had a perfectly good working front door, the keys to which were on a hook on the wall beside it.

Charlotte turned back to the bed. There was a scrap of paper lying innocently on it. She picked it up and unfolded it.

Sure enough, it was a note from Mediochre. To her.

Charlotte,
I'm sorry about the whole clichéd leaving-in-the-middle-of-the-night shtick, but I really can't stay. I hope you understand. You're a brilliant, intelligent girl and I'm sure you'd make an excellent dracologist, and I'm equally sure it would be a pleasure to tutor you.

Unfortunately, I can't. I can't afford to get attached to anyone like I think I may have been starting to get attached to you. It gets... confusing.
Have you ever tried living with the hormones of a teenager and the mind of a 50-year-old? Trust me: not fun. The flesh is willing but the spirit keeps lecturing it.

Anyway, maybe someday I'll find a way of overcoming this problem and then I'll be back. Until then, whatever you choose to do, I trust you'll do it well.

Dr Mediochre Quirinius Seth

***

At roughly the same time in the city of Vienna, a young woman was wandering aimlessly across an old stone bridge. There was nothing remarkable or eye-catching about her appearance. She was just one more brown-haired, freckled, slightly tanned British tourist is a crowd of similar tourists.

At a soft vibrating in her jacket pocket, the woman stopped and leant on the stone wall of the bridge to answer her mobile.

"Obsidian," said an expressionless, accentless voice from the other end of the line. Had anyone who knew the woman known this they would have been moderately confused, because she was known to the normal people she worked and lived with as Catriona.

"Topaz," the woman replied, leaning over the edge as if interested by something in the water below. "It worked, did it?"

"Oh yes," came the disembodied response. "Everything went as expected. The next part of this phase can begin whenever it is practical."

"Excellent," replied the woman who may have been called either Obsidian or Catriona. "I'm sure it will be so. I'll speak to you later then, if that's it."

"There is one unexpected detail which we have not yet accounted for," admitted her correspondent. "A girl. Possibly a new apprentice." The woman considered this news briefly.

"She can easily be written in," she concluded. "I'm sure it won't be a problem. You've done well. I greatly hope you will continue to do so."

"Of course, ma'am."

The woman whom most people referred to as Catriona smiled a little as she terminated the call, replaced the mobile, hoisted her backpack and began to walk towards a particular cathedral which she'd heard one had to see if one was visiting this city. Later that day *she* would be the one making a call to inform another of recent progress in the Tertiary Phase, but for now she had no reason to hurry.

In a large, sterile-looking room in a large, sterile-looking facility that couldn't be located on any road map or sat-nav, a large and sterile-looking man gave a large and sterile-looking corpse a final check-over, his gaze lingering on the torn-up chest, before ticking a small and not-particularly-sterile-looking box on a clipboard, and shoving the metal drawer in which the corpse lay closed.

In the darkness of the tiny, cramped drawer, just as the gorilla on the outside locked it and removed the key, the corpse could (had there been anybody to notice) have been seen to make the tiniest of spasms and emit a small moaning noise.

Had Mediochre been anywhere nearby with a piano, he could have told anyone who was interested that it was almost certainly due to gas escaping.

Almost certainly.

But that was not the ending...

Acknowledgements and Apologies

Every great novelist steals or borrows a lot of their material from friends, family and other writers. As it turns out, the rest of us do it too. So here's a list of some of the people who need to be thanked and/or apologised to after I used their work for, er, 'inspiration'...

Charlotte Campbell, who isn't really American at all, for a heroine who wasn't evil, old or a spinster.
Heather Penman, in association with the French, for missile bees.
Catriona Carter, for insisting I put her in somewhere.
Rowan Ingram, for mixing up 'so' and 'forth'.
Alastair Bartlett, for bizarre taste in names.
Kathryn 'Kaz' J, for permission to use you.
The anonymous Snapfax man, for having an effect on Charlotte that was, to say the least, amusing to observe.
And anyone else I may have based characters on or stolen ideas from.

Terry Pratchett, Douglas Adams, Eoin Colfer, Charlie Higson and Derek Landy, for writing style and the occasional pilfered plot detail.
J.D. Salinger, for clavichords.
Ludwig Van Beethoven fur Elise.
William Shakespeare, for general awesomeness.
Dr Ernest Drake's Dragonology for some general miscellaneous dracological background.
The Cast and Crew behind the A-Team, for loving it when a plan comes together.

Burns, Christie and the rest of Mediochre's reading list, for being the first writers that came to mind.

And anyone else I may have, erm, 'referenced'.

And, of course, there's the usual suspects:

Mum and Dad, for... you know... parenty stuff.

Eilidh, for, uh, moral support or something.

Kieran Sharkie, for still generally being Kieran

Lady, for accompanying me on the inspirational walks.

The staff of Firrhill High School, for, well, schooling.

Calum P Cameron, for putting in all the actual hard work and just being me.